THE MARK OF CANE

Short Stories from Trinidad

Kenneth Jaikaransingh

ISBN-13: 9798839975590
ISBN-10: 1477123456

Cover design by: Art Painter
Library of Congress Control Number: 2018675309
Printed in the United States of America

For Lisa and Dominic

PREFACE

I wish to thank all those who read early drafts of these stories, as well as those in my previous collection, who not only encouraged me along the way but helped me make useful and important revisions. These include my brothers Errol and Karl, my sister-in-law Tara, my cousin Ria and my former teaching colleagues Cheryl Mckenzie-Cook and Mervyn Mauricette. Cynthia Birch was an admirable and painstaking proof-reader.

This new collection moves backward and forward in time and place, from the canefields of early twentieth-century Trinidad to grainier and more urban settings. If they can be said to have a unifying theme, they deal immediately or remotely with the consequences of a colonial legacy, and the impact of that legacy on an island population, especially on the successive generations of Indian immigrants who first arrived in these parts primarily as indentured labourers, and came face to face with an alien and often unwelcoming environment.

Perhaps these stories will help remind us that the path to selfhood, individual or national, is bestrewn with diversions, cracks and falling rocks.

KJS, 2022

TABLE OF CONTENTS

TEA AND ROSES:
A PROLOGUE

Mrs Fairleigh was upset. She had complained in writing to the mayor several times about the nuisance from the establishment across the street. Every Friday and Saturday night she felt her sleep disturbed by the noise, whether African drumming, steelband or calypso. She understood that entertainment was an important part of the package offered to customers, especially foreign visitors keen on absorbing some local culture along with their dinner, but she didn't think it had to go on beyond midnight. And the garbage! In the morning, the drums they had put out for collection by the City Council scavenging trucks would be overflowing and stinking to high heaven if they hadn't been cleared by eight o'clock.

It hadn't been so two decades ago, she recalled. The Inn on The Green had been a respectable restaurant, offering afternoon tea and fine dining under the canopy of trees in its courtyard if one preferred to eat en plein air as opposed to the formal arrangement of tables inside. The entertainment then was provided by gentlemen in white dinner jackets playing the piano, or perhaps by a small quartet, or even a saloon singer or two. She had, as a young ingenue, attended several of the occasional parties held on special occasions; in fact, she had been swept off her feet at one such event by the handsome British naval officer who had later married her.

Now, however, with changed ownership, the Inn had taken on

a decidedly seedier character, and its clientele had changed as well. She noted with some disapproval the number of young coloured couples stepping out of hired taxis, still dressed to the nines but bringing a different kind of energy to the place. A few businessmen still dropped in, usually for lunch, but none of her contemporaries with whom she once waltzed, foxtrotted and merengued across the polished dancefloor ever seemed to go there anymore. They met instead, whenever they did, at the old Queen's Park Hotel across from the Savannah, where Scantlebury still served them gin and tonic, and lovely club sandwiches skewered together with specially commissioned toothpicks.

She knew, in fact, that she needed to move away from this neighbourhood altogether, perhaps to St Clair, Maraval, or one of the new exclusive developments being constructed west of the city. But she was reluctant to leave her house, this grand George Brown-designed building from the turn of the century, where louvred windows could be raised to let the morning sunshine in, where fine filigree work was evident on the iron rails of the fence, and where the fretwork on the wooden eaves testified to a skill few craftsmen now possessed. The entire living area was on the lower floor, but a highly polished staircase led to an attic where family heirlooms accumulated over decades were stored.

At the rear of the house, next to the small shed that served as the garage for her cream-coloured Triumph, she had carefully cultivated a variety of flowers, and from these had transplanted a series of teapot roses in varying hues to the front of the house, just behind her fence. These she nurtured diligently. Whenever Agatha came as she did twice a week to do the housework, she would find Mrs Fairleigh in her front garden, carefully pruning the stems or removing dead leaves and dying flowers, a broad straw hat on her head and gloves protecting her fingers from the thorns.

'Morning, Miss Lilian,' Agatha would say.

'Good morning, Agatha,' would come the reply. Agatha had done domestic duties for Lilian Fairleigh and her parents for over three decades and needed little guidance as to what household chores needed to be done.

'Is why you like them roses so, Miss Lilian?' Agatha once asked.

Miss Fairleigh stopped what she was doing and looked up at her.

'When my grandmother came to this country from England many years ago,' she finally said, 'she brought some rose cuttings with her. These roses come from those cuttings. So these roses are like part of my family history.'

'But who going to look after them when you gone, Miss Lilian? You don't have no children.'

Miss Fairleigh sighed. 'Yes, that's true. What will become of my roses? Perhaps my cousins will take over the house and the roses too.'

'You have cousins?'

'Distant cousins, really. Somewhere on my father's side. They come around sometimes.'

Agatha paused at the foot of the steps that took her up to her hillside home in the Cascade valley. The bus didn't come this far inside so she had to walk a further quarter of a mile from the terminus to the small community in which she had lived from childhood, except when her short-lived marriage had taken her away for a year and a half. She remembered too well the day when the taxi had stopped on the road and she had exited, looking up the hill and seeing her father standing there in his short khaki trousers and faded white undershirt, pitchfork in his hand and sweat staining his forehead.

'He send you back?' he asked, stabbing the pitchfork into the harsh unyielding soil.

'No, I leave,' she said. He grunted but said nothing further until they were both inside.

'When you having the child?' he asked, pointing to her stomach.

'Five months,' she said. 'I was hoping I could stay till the child born. Then I go look for a place to stay and a work somewhere.'

'You could stay as long as you want,' he said, then went into the small kitchen.

She never told him about the physical abuse, the threats and the infidelities, and he never asked. She occupied what used to be the room she had shared with her mother; her father had long taken to sleeping on the sofa in the living room, and never moved back into the bedroom, even after Mama died and Agatha had moved out. After Yolande was born, she had awakened one night to see her father sitting on a chair in the room, gazing blankly at the wall. When he too died some years later, she found herself all alone with a four-year old child to look after in this tiny shack hanging precariously from a hillside in Cascade.

Mr Stephens the shopkeeper told her one day that Luna, who worked as a domestic with Miss Harris down in the city, was going back to St Vincent and that Miss Harris was looking for a replacement. Was she interested in replacing Luna?

The interview with Miss Harris went well and she was on the job two days later, after making arrangements with a neighbour to look after Yolande during the day. Miss Harris was getting along in age, as was her husband Tony, but their daughter, Lilian, was about her own age. She had helped to comfort Lilian when news came that her husband had died in the war, then later as each of her parents passed away.

'I'll have tea in the morning room,' she called out to Agatha.

Agatha didn't reply but carried the tea tray into the designated 'morning room' at the back of the house, where the sun entered through the latticework and cast interesting shadows on the wall opposite. She stopped to look at the photograph of Captain Duncan Fairleigh, resplendent in naval uniform, with his bride Lilian Harris at his side. Poor man, she thought, didn't make it through the first engagement with the enemy.

She wondered briefly what had become of her own husband, Joseph, from whom she had not heard after she had left him and gone home. Perhaps he too had signed up and gone to war, she laughed fleetingly to herself, knowing how unlikely a possibility that was.

'Are you with the de Verteuils tomorrow?' Lilian asked. 'I can never remember what days you work with them.'

'Yes Miss Lilian. Mondays and Wednesdays I here, Tuesdays and Thursdays I with Miss de Verteuil.'

The de Verteuil home was just a few houses away from Miss Fairleigh's. It was that proximity in fact which had gotten her the extra job at that home. Miss Fairleigh associated with no one on the street but the de Verteuils; she did not like the fact that further up the street, some Indians from the country had recently moved in, adding to the already deteriorating character of the neighbourhood. This was once prime residential property, she thought silently; there were families like the Bermudez family, the Scotts and the Aleongs. Now a noisy primary school had been erected on the empty plot left after the Cobham residence had been torn down, and several coloured families now inhabited various sections of what had once been the Esmeralda Villas. Thank God, she thought, for the de Verteuils, and she was quick to recommend Agatha to their service when their own housekeeper had left.

'When you go tomorrow, please remind Mrs de Verteuil of our afternoon social next Friday. She and I are due to bring cucumber sandwiches and jam tarts.'

'Miss Lilian, you never thought about carrying things like small accra and float, or fishpies, things like that, to all you socials?'

'Heavens, no!' exclaimed Mrs Fairleigh. 'The ladies would be horrified if I brought along common food like that. What a terrible suggestion. Accras…indeed!'

Agatha continued wiping the dining table. Her eyes fell on the copy of the Trinidad Chronicle that lay on the side table.

'Miss Lilian, what you think about this Federation thing? You think all these islands could make it together?'

'Agatha, why do you keep asking me these foolish questions?' said Lilian, taking off her straw hat and gloves and coming inside. 'What do I know about politics?'

'Well, the Doc think is a good idea. He say we stronger when we together. And besides, Trinidad is the capital. We is number one.'

'The Doc?' inquired Miss Fairleigh.

'Doctor Williams. The Premier. If he say it go work, I agree with him. They say he is the third smartest man in the world, you know.'

'Really?' said Miss Fairleigh. 'Who are numbers one and two?'

'It had real people in the square last night. That man talk for two hours. Nobody move. You coulda hear a pin drop.'

'You go to political meetings, Agatha? I didn't know that.'

'Only recently, Miss Lilian. Since 1956. That man is a boss speaker, I tell you. He making black people feel proud again.'

'Yes, so I'm told,' said Lilian. 'Another messiah. Here to liberate the Jews.'

'Eh?' said Agatha. 'Anyway, he was on fire last night. The opposition DLP tie up with the Federal Party in Jamaica and they win the most seats. The Doc didn't like that. He say they only want to hold back progress.'

'Who?'

'Them Indians and them. I don't think he like the Adams man from Barbados either.'

'But he has several Indian people in his Cabinet? Why would he want to aggravate them by criticizing their people?'

Agatha shrugged her shoulders. 'He is the boss,' she said. 'He know what he doing.'

'Yes, I know,' said Lilian. 'The third smartest man in the world. Did you put my tea in the morning room as I told you?'

Miss Fairleigh sat in the morning room sipping her tea. She felt unusually uncomfortable, but it wasn't the weather, or the exertion she had expended on her roses. This was different, an uneasiness of the mind. She found herself recalling a conversation in her group a fortnight ago. Several of them were uneasy about the way things were shaping up. Those with a greater idea of world events talked about India and Kenya, and events in Egypt over the Suez Canal. Everywhere the order of things seemed to be under threat. The British Empire has fallen apart, said the wife of one diplomatic officer; soon we're going to be kicked out everywhere. What will happen then, said another, is that these people will begin fighting each other then themselves, scrambling to get to the top of the heap.

Miss Fairleigh didn't know much about these things, but what Agatha had said about the uneasy Federation arrangement and the attack on the Indian population disturbed her. Perhaps she might have to leave this wonderful house after all, she thought, perhaps go to England like the Walters from up the street had, or maybe Canada, which she had heard was beginning to attract emigrants from other countries. She took a sip of tea and looked out at the garden at the back. Weeds had begun to spring up, she noticed, and she would have to exercise caution removing them since they were lodging themselves tightly among the existing plants and flowers. Tomorrow perhaps, she thought, closing her eyes tightly, I'll deal with that tomorrow.

CROPTIME AT CONCORDIA

Mr Fletcher drove up in his horse and buggy, scattering clouds of dust from the unpaved road as he made his way to Ranjit's home. A few curious villagers stopped to look as he passed by. Transportation of this quality was scarce on the island, and even more scarce in this rural quarter. He had had the good fortune to have been allowed the use of this one, left behind by the estate owner who had come out briefly to look over his holdings then left within a fortnight on the steam packet, complaining of the heat, the mosquitoes and the smell, and hoping to catch a connection back to England as soon as he could.

Mr Fletcher guarded his good fortune tenaciously; it was rare for a manager to have had such luck with an employer. He himself had felt the same urge to leave immediately five years earlier when he had first come to the island seeking his fortune, but he had not had the wherewithal to afford his return passage, and after a torturous year as a clerk in the shipping company had been offered the position of manager on one of the company's many holdings by default, there being no suitable Englishman at the time willing and available to take the position.

He had known little then about sugar cultivation, and still did not. He was fortunate to have had Ranjit's services when he arrived. Ranjit was a rare find, an immigrant of some breeding who spoke English well, had served as boss driver on Concordia Estate for several years already, and knew sugar cultivation and processing intimately. When he asked Ranjit about his background and how he had learnt to speak English so well, Ranjit would demur except to say that he had been educated at an English grammar school in India when he was a child and interacted with Englishmen in India before crossing the waters with his father as a teenager.

Ranjit was at the hitching post where he had tied his horse when Mr Fletcher pulled up.

'Ah, Ranjit. Good morning. Just coming in, I see,' said Mr. Fletcher jovially.

'No, Mr Fletcher, heading out again. I was out earlier. Crop time start today, so the workers like to start before it get hot.'

'Yes, yes, of course, I forgot.'

The side door to Ranjit's house opened and his daughter came down the flight of stairs with several enamel cannisters clamped together by metal hinges in one hand, and a white cork hat in the other.

'Here, Pa. Ma send your tiffin and your helmet. Morning, Mr Fletcher.'

'Good morning, Radica,' Mr Fletcher replied. He looked the girl over quickly. She was pretty for an Indian, he thought, long black hair, lovely features, perhaps thirteen or fourteen years old; she would make some man a great wife shortly. He turned to Ranjit again.

'Captain Barker sent me a message from the city yesterday,' he said. 'Apparently workers on one or two estates are beginning to act up. He wants to know if you've noticed anything on our estate.'

Ranjit shook his head. 'Everything peaceful here, Mr Fletcher We have no trouble, nothing I notice.'

'There have been some disturbing incidents elsewhere, you

know. The authorities are concerned. Barker says that on one estate, the workers assaulted the driver. Even worse, there was a protest march from one estate to courthouse in the town nearby. That almost got out of hand. Now we are hearing about strikes on several estates.'

'I not hearing about anything. Everybody here working good,' said Ranjit.

'What about this fellow Bhola? He is one of your people, not so? His name was mentioned as one of the troublemakers.'

'Bhola don't do estate work no more,' said Ranjit. 'He have a joupa near Kandahar village,' said Ranjit, 'but is on his uncle land. I never know him to be no troublemaker.'

'Yes, but I hear he gathers the men together sometimes for meetings and such.'

'Is read he read for them most of the time, Badri tell me.' said Ranjit. 'From the Gita. The Ramayana. Holy books. Sometimes newspapers. He is Brahmin, a scholar. Most of the workers don't read or write, so that is a good help for them.'

'Righto, then,' said Mr Fletcher, returning to his carriage. 'I'm relieved to hear that. But I want you to keep a close eye on him. We can't have any unsettling business on Concordia. You will keep an eye out, won't you? Let me know if anything seems amiss. I'll tell Captain Barker that we're on top of things here. But I shall go see Bhola myself, what say you? Just to tell him to keep his hands clean and no silly business.'

Ranjit watched Mr Fletcher turn his carriage about, flick his riding crop and drive off at a canter, stirring up clouds of dust once more in his wake.

'Pa, you didn't hear something about trouble down Oropouche from Dindial?' asked his daughter, holding the horse as he mounted.

'Nah, Dindial like to exaggerate. Some confusion about wages or something. But I better go and see Badri tomorrow. Tell your mother I coming back after I check with the gangs them.'

Radica went upstairs to the kitchen after her father left. Her mother was washing dishes over the sink that projected from the windowsill over the backyard below, stacking them to dry on the wooden sideboard. Some ashes glowed in the nearby chulha. Ranjit had added a small annex off the main area for normal household cooking; his wife had complained about having to walk up and down a flight of steps in heavy rain.

'The aloo need peeling, child' said Jagdaye, pointing to the small heap of potatoes on the table. 'And I need some bhandanyia from the yard. You could do that for me, beti, while I go feed the animals? After that we could open the shop. '

The lower portion of the house had been converted into a small retail outlet, where Jagdaye stocked and sold a variety of items, dry goods, haberdashery, oil, whatever the passing salesmen brought for her and which she thought she could sell and make a small profit. The villagers flocked to her shop, for she sold on credit, recording each sale carefully in a worn pupils' exercise book that served as her accounting ledger, against which each buyer signed their name or made their mark. Accounts were settled in full when wages were paid at the end of the crop season, at which time the cycle would begin again. But Jagdaye would remind the village wives to settle outstanding accounts before their husbands had a chance to head to the rumshop with all the money in their pockets. She had herself thought of opening a small bar, but Ranjit had objected.

Radica enjoyed working in the shop. It gave her a chance to interact with the community in a way she would not normally have enjoyed. Her father disapproved silently of her presence in the shop, but after she had finished her primary schooling in the small Mission school, he recognized that she would be bored if she found nothing else besides housework to occupy her time.

But he still told her mother to keep an eye on her; women were still a prized commodity, and one with looks, education and the right caste such as his daughter would be greatly in demand when she came of age. He had already rejected several preliminary overtures from the parents of families in the area; he was determined that she would make a proper match.

Badri moved the hammock that was slung from the doorpost to a nearby tree and let Ranjit enter. 'Sit please, Ranjit bhai,' he said, pointing to a worn wooden chair. Ranjit took his helmet off and sat down. 'You want drink something?'

'A little water would be good,' said Ranjit. 'It hot and dusty outside.' Ranjit looked around. Badri had not done badly for himself, he thought, after leaving the estate. The money he had saved had gone a long way in helping him establish the small rice acreage that he had developed. Badri, he knew, also kept a few animals: a cow, two goats, the chickens that roamed freely on the dirt yard outside.

He took the enamel cup from Badri and drank.

'Is from the old copper outside dey,' Badri explained apologetically, finding nothing else to say. 'We does collect rainwater but we does boil it. The wife keep all the clean water in a pail over they.' He gestured towards the makeshift kitchen through the space that served as a window.

Ranjit nodded. 'We boil we own too,' he said. He handed the cup back to Badri. 'Badri bhai, I come to discuss something with you. You send for Bhola to come?'

Badri nodded.

'Mr Fletcher come by me to complain yesterday,' Ranjit continued. 'He say Bhola stirring up trouble on the estate them. You know anything 'bout that?'

Badri shuffled nervously. 'What kinda trouble him say?'

'Making workers restless. Talking about bad living conditions and such. Encouraging strike.'

'Well,' said Badri,' you know, him is big man. Not for me to tell big man what to do. Is your estate workers he dey with?'

'No, not my estate. Badri, you and me go back. We come on the same boat. This boy is your family. Is your job to talk to him.'

Badri took a sip of water from his cup. 'Ranjit bhai, is a problem I has to deal with here. The boy land here a grown man already. He is me sister bhatija, her husband nephew. His contract finish is one year now and since then stay here with me. But him nah able find work that he want. Him don't like field experience. Him went townside, they send him back after three days, say him don't want to work, him lazy, only want to read book. But I couldn't mind he forever.' He leaned over towards Ranjit. 'The wife complaining. And him was no help in the lagoon or with the animals either. I did ask you if it had anything you could find for he on your estate, remember? Checker? Tallyman? Him have education.'

Ranjit nodded. 'And I did ask why you wanted to send he by me? Estate work is hard work. You work estate yourself, you must know that,' said Ranjit. 'It have no place on estate for idle people, or people nah want to work. What you did expect me to say?'

'Him didn't mix too well with them others on them estate them. He is Brahmin. He didn't like dealing with them black gang boss specially. Them did make him feel not very welcome, always 'busing him and the others about devil-worship and nasty eating habits. I was hoping you did have something a li'l better for he.'

'Over here it have too much mix-up people. I never see that before I come here. White man, Chinee,Portogee. And so much black people. Them was slave and labourer before we. Now they getting pay, they think we come to take their work from them. Everybody dislike we. That is why we have to do we work and keep out of trouble.'

'That be true,' Badri agreed. 'Even we own people forgetting who they is and where them belong. It have no respect for your betters anymore, Ranjit bhai.'

'From the time we did land,' said Ranjit, 'like it didn't matter if you was Brahmin or not. Everybody working same place, using same tools, cutting same cane or digging same ditch. You self work in gang, had nobody did really know who was what. Nothing different now. Plenty Indian change their name when they come here. Some say they is Kshatriya; others say they is Brahmin. It have Parsi, Madrassi, Tamil... you remember when it had Mussulman on the estate with name like Mukherjee and Vishnudath?' said Ranjit. 'You could believe that? If Bhola think he could live like how he remember back in India, he fooling himself. We have to make do over here as best we could.'

'Well, lucky him had a little education. And he could manage good with the English he have. Him learn real quick.' He paused. 'Anyways, I put he in a small place I have near Kandahar Village. He does plant small garden, make him own way. Also teach people read and write, you know, add and take away. Simple thing. Read prayers for them. Him getting like a saddhu over there. Them what can't pay, them give him food and clothes.'

'Bhola lucky. When we did first come, some couldn't even talk to one another. It had some speak Bhojpuri, some Urdu, some Hindi. Now we all talking a little of the English, all of we,' Ranjit observed.

Badri said nothing. Ranjit scratched his chin. He and Badri had bonded as teenagers on the Sheila many years ago and had remained friendly. He had been happy for Badri when he finally left the estate and began small farming on his own; he liked to see a man prosper.

'You know, it have something else I did never tell you then,' said Badri, looking down at his feet. He paused for a moment. 'When the boy had was to leave India, the story is he leave to escape lock-up. So what you be telling me now 'bout making trouble, that bothering me a little bit.'

'What he do?' asked Ranjit.

'Well,' said Badri, 'him tell me it had some jhanjhat with the overseer dem in the village he from. Him had was to leave quick quick. But he never say why. That why I did eager find him someplace quick after contract, some place, you know, get him busy, start again...'

'So why now he getting heself mix up in trouble again? How long he here now, eight years? He is a born troublemaker or what? What it is he do back in the Bharat Mata?'

'Like I say, him never tell me. Bhola not he real name, you know' Badri whispered. 'That not him real name. Is what him put on the form in Kolkata.'

Ranjit was not surprised. 'Bhola. Innocent. Smart name to choose,' he said.

'Look the man self coming. You could ask him all your question direct,' said Badri, seeing Bhola coming into the yard, walking staff in hand and a small bundle over his shoulder.

Simon Fletcher brought his carriage to a halt at the Kandahar Village market to ask for directions.

'Over there,' said the elderly lady, pulling her ohrni closer around her head. 'Over there Bhola house. Half mile, maybe more. Him nah home, him gone Victoria Estate. Better sahib come back 'nother time.'

'No, it's all right,' said Fletcher smiling. 'It's just a social call.' The woman looked curiously at him but said nothing, turning her attention once again to the scattered vegetables laid out on the jute sack in front of her. Other vendors, all female, lowered their heads as he passed by. It was market day, he suddenly realised. Fletcher clicked his tongue, and his horse began trotting down the stone-hard dirt track, drawing the carriage behind. Cane swayed gently on each side of the track; their stalks were thick and full of juice, he thought as he watched the feathery plumes dancing above in the mildest breeze before inclining respectfully in his direction. A little further on, some patches of cane had already been cut, the stubble sticking stubbornly out of the trash of leaves left on the ground. Here and there an occasional ratoon had already sprung up, promising another harvest eventually.

His wife had gone to Port of Spain to visit her family. She complained constantly that she was fed up of life in the bush, and often departed for a week or two at a time, their daughter in tow, to spend with her parents, siblings and friends in the town. This time she had gone to take part in the masquerade parties popular in the week before Ash Wednesday; it was an opportunity to be reminded of that other self she had left behind when she had returned from finishing school in England.

Mr Fletcher was glad she had gone. He had thought that marrying into the local elite would have continued to provide him with elevated status among the locals, but she had found him out soon after their marriage, that he was not in fact the son of a London solicitor but of a common plumber and who, in desperate straits, had left London to make his way in the world by taking passage on a boat bound for the West Indies. She had treated him thereafter with a certain amount of marital disdain and kept him as far away from her family as she could.

Here, when she was away, he no longer felt belittled. He was a man again, not the object of abuse and derision as he was at home. Here he was treated with respect. People doffed their hats to him or gazed deferentially at the ground until he had passed; here the estate labourers called him 'Sahib,' like the Indians did, or 'Boss', as the few remaining Africans did, and turned to him for favours whenever they knew Ranjit would not accommodate them. He did, at times, just to emphasise that he was in fact the man in charge, but he really preferred to leave those matters to Ranjit's discretion and often referred them back to him with an apologetic shrug of his shoulders.

He pulled up outside what had to be Bhola's hut, a small structure with a jute sack instead of a door, curtainless windows. Parallel strips of bamboo enclosed the dirt -floored interior. In some places the walls smeared with the mixture of dried cowdung and dirt that he had now seen on so many peasant cottages; in others, tree branches had been used. A quilted patchwork of coconut palm branches and dried grass rested loosely on irregular rafters cut from trees. A bit like the thatched roofs back home, he thought, though not as sophisticated in their assembly.

The old vendor was right. Bhola was not at home. Mr Fletcher lifted the jute sack and took a step inside. The interior was surprisingly cool, he thought; occasional gusts of breeze swept through the solitary window, under the jute flap at the door or through crevices in the roof. A table, made of uneven planks nailed to a rough frame, occupied one side of the room. There were some books on the table. Mr Fletcher looked at them. Some were in Sanskrit, as far as he could make out, and seemed to be Hindu holy texts; there was a King James Bible as well, and leaflets from the East Indian National Association. On the other side of the room, two jute sacks had been sewn together and lay on the floor; a decorated enamel plate and a tin can stripped of any label rested next to a rolled-up heap of white cotton fabric.

He looked out the window. A small fireplace had been built in the yard, beyond which lay a small garden with a few bedraggled plants begging forlornly to be watered. There was a small clearing off to one side, which seemed to be more meticulously maintained and kept clean than elsewhere; another tin cup, with what looked like hibiscus flowers, rested on a small rough wooden table. Three bamboo poles decorated with coloured flags had been buried in the ground. Fletcher had seen these before. Jhandis, he said to himself, remembering the word. What a strange religion, he thought, full of quaint rituals and practices, and gods with multiple arms, animal features and skin of all colours. He had made a half-hearted attempt to understand it at times but given up in bewilderment.

He got into his buggy, tapped the horse with his riding crop and set off for home at a slow trot. He would come back to see Bhola in the morning. He felt instinctively that Bhola posed a threat to the tranquillity he enjoyed at Concordia.

'When your Pa say he coming back?' Jagdaye asked her daughter.

'He gone by Badri,' said Radica. 'He say he be back by nightfall. Estate business again, for sure.'

'Estate business, estate business, always estate business. Man should be looking for husband for you now, beti. You of marriage age. Nah can be too choosy.'

'Pa wouldn't marry me to any and everybody,' said Radica proudly. 'He think I too important.'

'Important, tcha! You too spoil. And is you Pa have you so. Maybe him gone by Badri to talk marriage with that boy was living dey, Badri nephew. He not a bad choice.'

'Who, Bhola?'

'You well know his name,' said Jagdaye.

'Well, he does come here in the shop to buy, not so? I must know his name.'

'And is sweet eye he does be making at you, and you making

back. Don't let your Pa catch you in this foolishness.'

'I don't make sweet eye with Bhola,' Radica protested. But there was something about Bhola that she did find fascinating. He was tall, with a deep sultry voice and piercing brown eyes. His black moustache gave him a distinguished look, she thought. She liked the way he persisted in wearing a dhoti, even though so many others were beginning to wear shirts and trousers in the island style. He was always clean. He never smelt of alcohol, or of the manure that hung about the feet and clothes of the labourers who came in every now and then. He read books, and often showed her what he was reading, taking it out from the bundle under his arm. Sometimes the books were in English; the holy books were in Sanskrit. He had offered to loan her one or two, but she had always declined. She was afraid that he would realise that her schooling had ended some time ago, and that she was also unable to read Sanskrit.

'But he nice, you don't think, Ma?' she blurted out.

'Nice looking nah mean nice person,' said Jagdaye. 'Him going land up in plenty trouble with police. Your Pa say he causing upset in them estate them.'

'What kinda trouble you talking about, Ma? '

'I hear he stirring up all the workers them with foolish talk. Ask your Pa when he come. He say Bhola making workers vex about pay and long hours, and how they living. Plenty kuchoor about no latrine, no doctor. Bhola better watch his tail. Straighten up the shelves. I going cook for your Pa. Lock up when you finish.'

'Mamoo. Sirdar, said Bhola, acknowledging both Badri and Ranjit. 'I come at a bad time?'

'No,no, ' said Badri. 'Ranjit here want to discuss something with you, Bhola bhai. Best you sit down. Some water?'

Bhola declined. Ranjit stroked his chin.

'Listen, bhai,' he began slowly, 'Mr Fletcher come by me yesterday. Say you among those encouraging workers to misbehave. That is true?'

'I ain't no troublemaker, Sirdar. All I does do is read the holy books for them and listen to their problems. You know that.' He opened his bundle and showed them the copy of the Gita he was carrying.

Ranjit nodded. 'When you say listen to their problems, what exactly you mean?'

'Well, they have plenty complaints 'bout long hours, bad pay, sickness, bad conditions. It not easy for them on the estate. You seeing that yourself, not so?'

'Well, we shouldn't meddle in that, you know. It have a Estates Inspector for that. That is the man to hear they complaints.'

Bhola laughed. 'You not serious, Sirdar. Estate Inspector come by is once in a blue moon. And even when him come, is no guarantee anything going to improve. Plenty complaints about malaria and other sickness on Campbell estate. It have a few dead last year. Nothing change. Is like they want us to dead so they wouldn't have to pay wages.'

'Maybe you right. Maybe things need to improve. But we have to be careful. The police fierce these days. They catch you off the estate without pass, is lock-up and fine. They very 'fraid these days. It have a big war going on outside. They don't like hearing 'bout strike and demonstration and violence right now. They extra nervous.'

'Is more than just that, Sirdar. Is not now we people getting pressure. Long time they want to change we. They using all kinda excuse to mash up we religion, we language, we customs. You not seeing how them missionaries turning people into teacher and Church minister? Is a plan to make Indian people forget everything they have.'

'Maybe you right,' said Ranjit, 'but provoking them only going to cause riot in the place.'

'You remember the Hosay when we did just land?' Badri intervened. 'Plenty people dead.'

'I remember damn good,' said Ranjit. 'My father was in that procession. Plenty like him wasn't Mussulman. But they was enjoying the celebration. Then the police begin to shoot.'

'Your father get shoot?' asked Bhola.

'No, he was lucky. But he see one of his friends get hit in his chest with a bullet. It make him sick.'

'So you should know what I talking 'bout,' said Bhola. 'Is real injustice in this place.'

'Yes, it unjust. But I learn from my father. You have to learn to work around these people if you want to live and make yourself better. You can't fight them; them have all the power. What you have to do is learn all you could from them, so that you ready when the time come. The only way to do that is to co-operate, until you get some power yourself.'

'Like you, you mean, Sirdar,' said Bhola with a touch of bitterness. 'That easy for you to say. You have nice house, family, little business. You is a overseer on the estate. You not struggling like most people, fighting to make a living, living in bad conditions and not getting proper pay for their labour. Is real advantage they advantaging us.'

'I didn't reach where I reach by avoiding hard work or encouraging mischief. All you doing is making things worse, for yourself and everybody else. Look,' said Ranjit, leaning closer to Bhola, 'you have to be careful. I hear you had some trouble back in the old country. You don't want to encourage no investigation, you hear me? We is still outsiders in this country.

The white people don't like us. Neither the black people. In them eyes, we taking bread from they mouth. The best thing we could do is, well, live quiet and stick to weself. Live how they expect us to live but grow stronger on the side. Learn from them how best to go forward.'

Badri was nodding slowly as Ranjit spoke. Bhola picked up his walking staff and retied his bundle.

'Sirdar, I respect you, and I think you do good for yourself. You too, Mamoo. But I have my work to do too. I have to help my people hold on to what is theirs before they forget where they come from and who they is. I appreciate the warning you passing on, Sirdar; I will make sure not to encourage any violence. But I not able to control how people feel about things sometimes.'

He turned to leave.

'You need anything? Badri asked anxiously.

'No, I alright, Mamoo. It getting late, and I don't want to rh home in the dark.'

Radica suddenly realized that it had grown dark outside. She closed the shutters and put the wooden bars across them, then went to the door. Someone suddenly slipped through the doorway.

'Close the door, girl, and lock up quick, 'said Bhola, moving to help her. Then he blew out the lamp she had lit some minutes before.

'What wrong, Bhola?' she asked, suddenly nervous.

'I hiding whole evening in that canefield behind the house,' he said. 'I think the police must be looking for me by now.'

'The police? What you do?'

'I didn't do nothing. Fletcher fall from he buggy and hit he head.

I leave him there on the ground.'

'But how that have anything to do with you?' asked the bewildered girl

'Well, it complicated. He was driving on the road, we meet, we exchange words. He raise his whip to hit me. I raise my stick, the horse get frighten and raise up, the carriage turn over and Fletcher fall and hit he head.'

'He dead?'

'No, was breathing when I leave, but a small cut on he forehead, was bleeding. I think he hit a stone on the ground. But you know what going to happen.'

'What is that?'

'You can't touch white people in this place. They go say I attack him. He go say so too. That is lock up for people like me.'

'But you didn't do nothing. You say you ain't touch him.'

'That's what I say. That's what I know. But the story going to come out different when he tell it. I have to get away from here. Run in the forest or something. They not going to let no Indian even think he could assault a bossman, far less a white man.'

'But you could tell the truth. They can't lock you up for telling the truth.'

Bhola snorted derisively. 'Look, I want some provision to help me out. What you have? A little rice, salt, some salmon, biscuit, sugar. Anything else? What about a little coffee or tea?'

He was grabbing things off the shelf as he spoke. 'You have something to put these in?' He grabbed one of the empty Farmers Mill flour sacks that Jagdaye had washed and stored neatly under the counter. 'This will do. What about money? I not stealing, I borrowing. I going to pay back when I could. Look, you could take anything you find in me joupa.'

'Ma done take any cash she had upstairs,' said the girl. 'I wouldn't interfere with her money anyway. That is really stealing.'

Bhola hesitated. 'What about that bera you have on there? That is gold, not so? Give me that, then.'

'My grandmother give me that when she was dying,' Radica protested. 'I can't give you that.'

Bhola hesitated. 'I sorry. I will pawn it and get some money. I will get it back for you later.' He held her wrist and took the bracelet off. 'I going now. Don't tell nobody I was here.' He turned to her before he got to the door. 'You is a good child. I was hoping to talk to your father about marriage sometime.'

He opened the side door cautiously, looked from side to side, and saw no one. He pushed the door back in and darted off in the direction of the canefield.

'Who that was?' said Ranjit, appearing suddenly at the side door. He had been standing briefly on the landing at the top of the staircase listening to the voices in the shop before descending. 'That was Bhola? What going on here?'

Mr Fletcher pulled up outside Ranjit's house. The only sign of his misadventure two weeks earlier was a faint scar above his right eye. A black policeman carrying a rifle had come with him, seated on the rear luggage rack at the rear of the buggy. He came down quickly from the buggy when it stopped.

'Good evening, Ranjit. All is well?' asked Mr Fletcher

Ranjit nodded. 'Glad to see you up and about, Mr Fletcher. You come back quick from town.' The policeman made him uneasy.

'Yes, Mrs Fletcher thought I should stay for a while after I went to the hospital. She didn't want me to come back, you know. This is Corporal Quashie from Couva Police Post,' Mt Fletcher explained. 'He want to talk to you about Bhola.'

'Bhola? What I could know about Bhola? Ain't he off hiding in the bush somewhere? Is not more than a fortnight now he disappear?'

Radica and her mother emerged from the shop where they had been arranging the shelves. Neither said anything.

'Oh, you didn't know? They caught him a few days ago. In the forest. I better let Quashie here tell you more about it. He was part of the team that caught him. Quashie?'

Ranjit said that he didn't know. Radica was startled. She saw her father looking at her and quickly regained her composure.

'This sack, overseer, you know anything about this?' The corporal produced an off-white flour sack with words printed on it.

Ranjit shook his head.

'People say your wife does sell flour from sack like this. Is true?'

Jagdaye spoke for the first time. 'Plenty shop, they sell-um flour from bag like that. Is how all the flour come. Is a Farmers Mill bag.'

'Yes,' said Mr Fletcher, 'but the police are curious. Yours is the only shop in this area for miles around. They are thinking it must have come from your shop.'

"My wife does give away plenty sack like that,' said Ranjit. 'Where you get that?'

'We find it by Bhola when we pick him up,' said Corporal Quashie. 'He was using it to carry what little belongings he had.'

'Belongings?' asked Ranjit.

'Yes, he had some things with him. A book, a soap, some matches... in fact, is some smoke from a fire he light in he lean-to that make we spot him,' said Quashie. 'What about this?' He reached into his pocket and pulled out something wrapped in a handkerchief.

Jagdaye recognized the bera immediately. She turned sharply to her daughter but saw Ranjit's restraining hand up and stopped. Radica suddenly felt very faint.

'Is a bera. Plenty Indian women have bera, Corporal. Is like a family jewel,' Ranjit replied. 'That one look like plenty others I see.'

'That's right, Corporal,' said Mr Fletcher. 'Indian people here believe in keeping their wealth in gold jewelry. I have seen quite a few like that.'

'The thing is,' said Corporal Quashie, 'Bhola was wearing it on he wrist. That unusual. When we ask him where he get it, he say was a lady friend give him. But nobody know Bhola to have any lady friend. He did live alone. You know any lady friend he have who like him so much to give him this expensive bracelet?'

'I didn't know Bhola very good,' said Ranjit. 'You talk to his uncle? Badri?'

'Long time. Badri don't know nothing 'bout it. Badri say he hardly see Bhola. In fact, last time was when you and he had a talk with him, same day he assault Mr Fletcher.'

'Yes,' said Ranjit. 'I remember. That was about a month ago.'

'What about you, Miss Ranjit? You know anything 'bout this bracelet?' Quashie had noticed Jagdaye's reaction when he had produced the bera. 'Or you, girl?' he continued, turning to Radica. 'You two does deal with all the women in this area. All you ever notice this on anybody hand?'

They both shook their heads. Radica noticed that her mother's lips had been reduced to a thin line, and her jaw firmly set.

'I don't think there's anything here,' said Mr Fletcher. 'Ranjit and his family are important people in this area. Ranjit, as I told your Inspector, has been a loyal servant to this estate for over twenty-five years. There has never been the slightest doubt about his loyalty to the estate, the Crown or to me. I think we could look elsewhere for information.'

The corporal nodded, put the flour sack back in his bag. He wrapped the bera once again in the handkerchief, put it in his pocket, then sat once again on the luggage rack of the buggy. Mr Fletcher raised his riding crop to start the horse.

'Mr Fletcher,' Radica suddenly blurted out. 'What going to happen to Bhola now?' She avoided her mother's eyes.

'Well,' said Mr Fletcher, 'he will go before the court charged with assault. They will find him guilty. Also, he tried to evade answering for the assault, so I assume he will get a few months. You know, Ranjit,' he said, turning to her father, 'it look like Bhola is not his real name. I hear is Purohit or something like that. Apparently, he was involved in some crime back in India.'

'What crime that was?' asked Ranjit.

'Well, I'm not really sure. Captain Barker thinks it had something to do with attacking a village overseer. Serious wounding, maybe worse. They've sent for the documents. Those won't be here for some while, I think. But if he committed some serious crime in India, more than likely they will try him here for that too. The British Government can't let crime go unpunished.'

He turned the buggy around, then stopped again.

'By the way, Ranjit, you're going to have another manager shortly. Mrs Fletcher insisted that I give up this job and return to England with her and Margaret. I don't expect to be here longer than a fortnight or so more. The new man should be out by then. I'll drop by to say goodbye before I leave.'

He flicked his riding crop, and the horse and buggy moved off kicking up its usual cloud of dust. Corporal Quashie, seated on the luggage rack facing them, waved as they trotted away. Ranjit turned to his wife and daughter. No one spoke. They climbed the staircase slowly. As he walked up, Ranjit noticed that a few of the wooden treaders had become loose, nails no longer holding them securely in place. I'll fix those later, he said to himself. As he got to the landing, he heard his wife quarreling loudly with his daughter inside. He stood for a while, not really listening, his mind elsewhere. He was glad he had passed by Bhola's hut and secured his books and other belongings the week before. He inhaled deeply; the scent of recently-cut cane filled his nostrils. Then he went inside.

A TERM OF TRIAL

Port of Spain, Trinidad

4 September

Dear Mam and Da

I have finally arrived in Trinidad. The flight from Dublin via London was long and exhausting, so I was quite relieved to spend the first two or three nights in a hotel here in the capital city before I go to my arranged lodgings which I am told are some distance away.

The weather here is quite humid, hot in the mornings followed by heavy rain in the afternoon. The shower that fell yesterday was quite unlike anything we see back home.

This being my first travel outside Ireland, I find Trinidad very unusual in many respects. I am surprised by the mixed population, especially the number of black and Asian people. On the drive in from the airport, I found the sides of the main road quite cluttered with houses. Near Port of Spain itself, there is a neighbourhood of sorts that doesn't quite seem to belong to a capital city, and a large dump apparently just across from it.

My first day begins day after tomorrow, and I am quite looking forward to it.

Love to Kate and Deirdre and all the neighbours

Your loving son

Liam

FROM THE OFFICE OF THE PRINCIPAL

TO: All Staff Members

DATE: 6 September

I take this opportunity to welcome you all back most heartily to the start of a new school year and a new school term. I especially welcome all new members of staff, in particular Mr Liam Kelly who joins us from Ireland. I know we are all looking forward to ensuring that the pupils in our charge benefit not only from the quality of instruction that we always provide, but to the added value provided by a good Catholic education.

Class assignments have already been handed out and placed on your desks. Please see the Librarian to collect any textbooks you may need for the classes to which you have been assigned.

In addition to your class assignments, I have also made the following appointments:

Mrs Scott : Music and Choir

Mr Dalrymple : Cultural Activities

Mr Kalloo : Sports Master

Other appointments will be made as the term goes by. The Deans appointed in the last schoolyear will continue in their positions.

Please note that our first staff meeting has been scheduled for Wednesday at 2.30 pm. Afternoon classes will be shortened by ten minutes to accommodate this. The agenda for this meeting will be:

1.Should Lower 6 Students be automatically promoted to Upper 6?

2.A review of the rules and regulations of the school, with a view to improving discipline in all areas.

3.Should parents have the right to take their sons out of school at any time?

4.'Personal problems' that seem to affect staff and their performance.

5.A dress code for staff

Fr Arthur Brady, Principal

FROM THE OFFICE OF THE PRINCIPAL

10 September

MINUTES OF THE STAFF MEETING HELD 8 SEPTEMBER, 2.30 pm

1. Fr Principal welcomed everyone to the start of the new term and the new school year. He expressed optimism that the year would be productive and rewarding for all.

2. Fr Principal went through his shortlist of what he expected from all members of staff. These included arriving on time for the start of classes, respect by staff for the authority of the school Principal, the absolute necessity for discipline among our students, for which the example must be set by the teaching staff, and the importance of Catholic principles in our student population.

3. Fr Principal indicated that he had decided that parents could only remove their sons from the school premises with the express permission of the Principal, which must be given in writing.

4. Fr Principal said that he understood that teachers would sometimes have personal problems or domestic duties but urged teachers to find ways to minimize any possible impact on their

ability to look after their classes efficiently.

5. Fr Principal presented a comparative chart he had prepared which showed that our student performance at national examination level had been drastically declining over the past few years. He noted in particular that we were no longer winning national scholarships in the numbers for which the school had always been renowned and said that several past students had been telling him that this was because the school no longer had a sizeable enough proportion of teaching priests. He emphasized that he knew the staff would do everything in their power to show that this was an unwarranted criticism. He however read from a letter he received during last year as follows:

"I am aware that we cannot expect the devotion of the average lay teacher to match the devotion of a dedicated priest. If the standard of work at Holy Saviour's is seen as deteriorating, it is easy to see that this will not be blamed on the Fathers but on the fact that the number of priests at the College has decreased and the number of lay teachers increased.It is important to show that high standards can be maintained with a predominantly lay staff, and that the devotion of the average lay teacher can indeed match the devotion of a dedicated priest."

The meeting concluded at 2.50 pm.

Carole O'Connor, Secretary to the Principal

12th September

Dear Mam and Da

How are you both? I hope in good health.

I have had my first week at this school. It is a fairly big school, and one of the best in the country, if I am to judge by what people have been telling me since I arrived on the island last week. I am still surprised by this country and by this school. I have never seen such a mixed group of people in any one place, all races and skin colours, even on the staff. Some are really strange mixtures of races. They have all been very pleasant and welcoming, however.

It is all of course very new to me, but I am really glad I took this exchange teacher program when it was offered. I'm having a few problems with my accommodation, and am still at the hotel, but I know this will be sorted out shortly.

Love to Deirdre, Kate and everybody

Your loving son,

Liam

.

20 September

Dear Fr Brady

I have been asked by members of the teaching staff to ask you for an explanation as to why you have asked students to write down the time that their classes begin and to submit this information to you on a daily basis.

As you must be fully aware, having students 'report' on teachers is guaranteed to undermine the very discipline you have been asking for, since it not only pits students against teachers but offers considerable opportunity for aggrieved students to embarrass or otherwise land teachers whom they do not like into administrative difficulties.

You will note that I have seen no need to mention that this is not just an affront to the dignity of a teacher; it creates a polarization between the lay staff and the student population that cannot bode well for the school culture and relationships within it.

Yours respectfully

Thomas Taylor, Senior Staff Representative.

FROM THE OFFICE OF THE PRINCIPAL

21 SEPTEMBER

NOTICE: PUNCTUALITY

TEACHERS ARE REMINDED THEY SHOULD BE IN CLASS BEFORE THE PRAYER IS SAID AT 8.05 AM AND 12.50 PM. ON 18 SEPTEMBER NINE (9) TEACHERS WERE LATE IN THE MORNING AND THIRTEEN (13) WERE LATE IN THE AFTERNOON. ON 19 SEPTEMBER, NINE (9) WERE AGAIN LATE IN THE MORNING.

PLEASE NOTE THAT WITH IMMEDIATE EFFECT, IN THE CASE OF ANY TEACHER WHO IS LATE, AN " L" IN RED WILL BE PLACED AGAINST HIS OR HER NAME IN THE REGISTER, AND HE OR SHE MUST WRITE A REASON FOR BEING LATE IN THE REMARKS COLUMN.

FR ARTHUR BRADY, PRINCIPAL

26 September

Dear Mam and Da

I am sorry not to have written earlier but things have been really hectic here.

I am enjoying my classes. I find the students very lively and quite intelligent. Some of them could make it on to university quite easily in the near future. I do have difficulty with the local dialect, however, and cannot quite understand what they are saying sometimes. I believe they often make fun of me, but not in an offensive manner. A student yesterday told me that I walked like a bullerman; I initially thought he was referring to my agricultural roots, but other students laughed uproariously when I mentioned it to them. I suspect I shall have to check out the phrase discreetly.

I haven't yet sorted out the accommodation problem I mentioned either. Because there was a last-minute change in the original exchange arrangement, I am now staying in a very rural area called Coalmine Village, and I have no hot water available.

I also have to get up very early to take two taxis to get to Port of Spain where the school is located. I don't mind getting up early but having to share with 3 or 4 strangers in a small car can be very uncomfortable, especially with the horrendous traffic on the road in this small island. Fr Brady has said he is trying to fix my accommodation issues with the local Ministry of Education.

There are one or two rumblings at the school among the lay staff, I hear. I sit next to Dr Wharton, a retired former lecturer who is teaching on a pension, and he tells me that teachers are complaining about the autocratic way in which the school is being run. But, he says, that's how the school has always been run.

Quite a few teachers are also complaining about having students report to the principal when they arrive for class. I have to agree that I find that very disconcerting as well.

I hope you are both well. Love to Deirdre and Kate.

Your loving son,

Liam.

3 October

Fr A Brady

Principal

Dear Fr Brady

Please note that I take a very dim view of your actions this morning when you attempted to have students lift my car out of the way to allow guests to depart the school premises. As you are fully aware, I was parked in my assigned parking spot, duly indicated by my having painted my licence plate numbers clearly on the ground. Your guest chose to disregard this, and parked there, forcing me on arrival to park immediately behind them.

Your attempt to have students lift my car out of the way so that your guests could then depart is a major breach of etiquette, not to mention the potential damage that could have resulted to my vehicle. Had I not been in a nearby classroom and alerted to developments, I would have been unable to have the students desist.

Your subsequent re-appearance on the scene and attempts to have students proceed with their course of action was again only stopped by my returning and advising you and students to desist or risk being sued.

I consider your actions another ill-advised step in your ongoing attempts to undermine the authority of teachers in this school.

Yours sincerely

Linda Harripersad, Teacher II

cc Senior Staff Representative

4 October

From: Fr R de Boissiere, Dean of Discipline

To: Fr A Brady, Principal

Please be advised that on yesterday's Student Noticeboard, I observed that Mr Kalloo has named Akeem Ali captain of the school's First Eleven Football team.

Quite apart from the disciplinary issues that Ali has had with me since the school term began, it cannot be fitting that a practising and fervent Muslim student be allowed to captain as prestigious a team as the Football First Eleven.

Your urgent intervention is requested.

R d B.

FROM THE OFFICE OF THE PRINCIPAL

TO: MR J.KALLOO

7 OCTOBER

DEAR MR KALLOO

PLEASE BE KIND ENOUGH TO NOMINATE ANOTHER PLAYER IN PLACE OF AKEEM ALI AS CAPTAIN OF THE FIRST ELEVEN TEAM. YOUR CO-OPERATION IS APPRECIATED.

Fr Arthur Brady, Principal

FROM THE OFFICE OF THE PRINCIPAL

TO: MR J KALLOO

9 OCTOBER

DEAR MR KALLOO

DESPITE MY WRITTEN INSTRUCTION TO YOU TO REMOVE AKEEM ALI AS CAPTAIN OF THE FOOTBALL TEAM, IT HAS BEEN REPORTED TO ME THAT YOU ALLOWED AKEEM ALI TO WEAR THE CAPTAIN'S ARMBAND IN YESTERDAY'S INTER-SCHOOL REPRESENTATIVE MATCH.

PLEASE BE KIND ENOUGH TO SEE ME IN MY OFFICE TO EXPLAIN.

Fr Arthur Brady, Principal

FROM THE OFFICE OF THE PRINCIPAL

TO ALL MEMBERS OF STAFF

11 OCTOBER

PLEASE BE ADVISED THAT I HAVE REPLACED MR J KALLOO AS SPORTS MASTER. MR D AUSTIN HAS BEEN ASKED TO ASSUME RESPONSIBILITIES AS SPORTS MASTER.

Fr Arthur Brady, Principal

Fr A Brady, Principal

Holy Saviour College, Port of Spain

11 October

Dear Fr Brady

After long and careful consideration of the dismissal of Akeem Ali as captain of the First Eleven Football Team, and his subsequent suspension from the school, I regret I have no choice but to resign as coach of the school team with immediate effect.

I have been coach of the school teams for over five years. In that time, I have coached Akeem Ali as a player and have always found him polite, interested and of clear leadership potential. In fact, he has successfully captained under-14 and under-16 teams on my watch and has had the total respect of his teammates at all times.

It seems most unusual to me that a student of his calibre, who wears the school monogram on his shirt, should be deprived of the First Eleven's captaincy on the basis of his faith and seemingly spurious allegations of indiscipline as reported to me by several of his teachers.

I have advised the players and Mr Kalloo of my decision.

I regret this decision but must do as my conscience dictates.

Yours sincerely

Richard Smith.

13 October

Dear Fr Brady

The Teaching staff has asked me to write to you formally, following our face-to-face discussion yesterday, about your handling of the Akeem Ali matter and related issues.

With respect to Ali, we wish to point out that this student has always had excellent grades, has not been a disciplinary problem, and has not only captained school teams since he was fourteen, but is the most experienced player on the team, one respected by his teammates. It seems contradictory that he should not now be allowed to captain the First Eleven team. It further beggars belief to learn that you have now suspended him from attending classes.

If, as has been suggested, all this is due to his faith, this too goes against the grain not only of reward via merit, but it also contradicts the history of Holy Saviour's in the past three or four decades of welcoming students of all faiths and backgrounds, and the reality that non-Catholic students have been consistently winning both academic and non-academic prestige for the school in many disciplines.

It seems to us that the existence of a Parent-Teachers' Association, which you and the school   administration have so long resisted, might have been an ideal vehicle for resolving issues such as this. The Student Council, which you so arbitrarily dismissed last term alleging that it was fomenting dissent among the students, might also have proved an invaluable resource at this time.

The staff has asked me as well to raise your ongoing failure to engage with its members on such matters as the hiring of new staff, disciplinary measures within the school, and other critical matters involving school policy. You have a staff populated by individuals who not only possess academic credentials but have considerable educational and life experiences which should be maximized for the benefit of the school, not slighted or ignored.

Your tendency to write directly and immediately to the Ministry of Education whenever there is some disagreement between yourself and any staff member, and the latent threat reported to us that members of your administration are suggesting even further punitive action in certain matters have also become issues of grave concern.

We look forward to constructive engagement with you on these and other matters in the future.

Yours sincerely

Thomas Taylor, Senior Staff Representative.

RESTORE STUDENT DEMOCRACY NOW!!

The dark agents of the reactionary forces in the College have struck again! This time the victim is Akeem Ali. The powers-that-be have objected to his captaincy of the First Eleven, claiming that he is a disciplinary problem.

This is not so! Akeem Ali has an unblemished disciplinary record, but he is being targeted not only for his outspoken views, but because the school authorities cannot accept a Muslim as a school captain in a Catholic School.

This is unacceptable! Students of all faiths have attended Holy Saviour's for many years and have won scholarships and other honours for the school since they were admitted.

This issue goes beyond Akeem Ali. We have witnessed a consistent attempt by the school administration to deny students representation and/or participation in school affairs which affect us directly. The Students' Council has been dissolved. Student publications are being censored prior to distribution. Student views are being ignored!

We as students must not aid and abet repression in school and elsewhere. We must never be accomplices in undemocratic, authoritarian practices. We must call on the repressive clique to cease the victimization of progressive students NOW!

Stand up on principle, for things will certainly get worse.

The Students' Democratic Press.

The Chronicle, 15 OCTOBER

SHUT DOWN AT HOLY SAVIOUR COLLEGE !

(Reporting by David Webb)

Classes came to a screeching halt at Holy Saviour College yesterday as students protested noisily against the dismissal of Akeem Ali as captain of the First Eleven football team.

Displaying placards and chanting 'Akeem, no, he must not go!', students milled about on the college premises, refusing to go to classes.

Ali was dismissed as captain then suspended from school by the School Administration for allegedly flouting an instruction from the Principal to resign the position.

Sources from the school say that Mr John Kalloo has also been dismissed from his position as sports master at the school.

The Chronicle understands that while the demonstration was organized by the Student Council, there is considerable support for the students' position by members of the Teaching Staff, who also feel that Ali has been victimized.

Efforts to contact the school Principal for comment have been unsuccessful.

16 October

To the parents of students at Holy Saviour College

The teaching staff writes to inform you and seek your support in a matter it considers crucial to the welfare and survival of Holy Saviour College as an educational institution.

At a meeting of the staff yesterday 15 October, a decision was taken that teachers will embark on a work-to-rule protest at the school in order to highlight many of the issues that have been affecting performance, morale and relationships at Holy Saviour. Teachers will, until further notice, report to their classes as assigned but carry out no teaching duties until these matters have been properly addressed by the school's administration.

The catalyst for our action has been the removal as captain of the School First Eleven and subsequent suspension of Akeem Ali, an outstanding Form 6 student. The student has been further informed that he will no longer be able to represent the school in any activity. Efforts are being intensified to portray Ali as having a history of disciplinary problems, of being an agitator and of propagating tenets of the Muslim faith in the school. We are prepared to demonstrate that most of this has no substance whatsoever. We also consider it unfair that Ali is being denied not only a hearing in this matter, but that his opportunity for completing his studies and potentially pursuing higher education is now seriously jeopardized.

This however is not an isolated issue. Over the past two years, a clear pattern of suppression of freedom of opinion and victimization of individuals involved has emerged, in both the student and teaching population. Extensive coverage of these matters will be included in a memorandum currently being prepared for the attention of the School Board and the Ministry of Education.

While you will naturally be concerned about the education of your son, we emphasise that the action being taken within the context of broader events shall provide students with a rich learning experience not easily found in the classroom.

We know after careful consideration, you will add your voice to ours among those calling for improvement in the management of Holy Saviour.

Yours very sincerely

Thomas Taylor, Senior Staff Representative

The Chronicle, 17 OCTOBER

TEACHERS STRIKE AT HOLY SAVIOUR'S

(reporting by David Webb)

Teachers at prestigious Holy Saviour's College have gone on strike.

In a letter to parents of students at the school, a copy of which The Chronicle has received, the teaching staff advise parents that they will be working strictly to rule. They shall attend classes but do no teaching.

This is the latest twist in a saga that began a week ago with the removal of Akeem Ali as captain of the school football team, and his suspension from the school. The teachers' action follows a student boycott of classes last week following Ali's suspension.

Attempts to reach both Mr Thomas Taylor, the Senior Staff Representative, and Fr Arthur Brady, the school's Principal, for comment have been unsuccessful.

The school has requested a postponement from the Schools' League in its fixture this week against St James Secondary.

17 October

To; Fr A Brady, Principal

From: Fr R de Boissiere, Dean of Discipline

Please be advised that as per your instructions I have spoken to the parents of Anthony Fernandez, Neil Gillespie and David Sookram, advising them that their sons will be suspended from school for seven days, having been identified as the ringleaders of last week's student chaos in the school.

Their official letters of suspension have been placed on your desk for your signature.

RdB

18 October

Dear Mam and Da

I moved out of the country place, as you suggested, and took a studio apartment in the town. I'm paying for it out of my own pocket, but I am now so much more comfortable, and arrive early every day. In fact, I arrived early the other morning to see it raining books! Well, not really, but Fr Brady had students throwing old books from a private library two floors up onto the big yard below! Amazing. Can you imagine throwing books away so carelessly? One that I picked up was a 1920 edition of Robinson Crusoe.

The situation in the school appears to be worsening day by day. I am now beginning to wonder whether I did the right thing by signing on for this Teacher Exchange program. I certainly thought that Holy Saviour's, being a Catholic school with a long tradition, was an easy fit for me but this school appears to have certain problems associated with it that I didn't realise when I came here.

One thing I didn't know when I signed on was that although this is a Catholic school, boys of all religions attend, something which we don't have back home. There are Hindus, Muslims, a few Jews; it's all very strange to me. The same with the teachers. It still takes some getting used to. What is happening in the school is actually over a dispute involving a Muslim student.

Another thing is that although the school has been run by priests for such a long time, people are beginning to feel that it is time for lay people to take over. There aren't so many priests around, anyway, so that might happen eventually, although I feel Fr de Boissiere is very keen to become Principal. He is local, so that puts him in a very good spot.

There has been a big disruption in the school this week. The students boycotted their classes a few days ago in support of the problem student. The teachers have now voted to go to classes but not teach; over here they call it work to rule. I am in a quandary, wondering what I should do.

Thank you for the package you sent. I enjoyed looking at the pictures. The countryside looks so green and inviting, and I'm beginning to miss our farm, the fieldstone fences and the rolling hills I see in those pictures. It's raining buckets over here, just like home.

The bottle of Bushmills whiskey is deeply appreciated.

Your loving son

Liam

FROM THE OFFICE OF THE PRINCIPAL

TO ALL MEMBERS OF STAFF

19 OCTOBER

I have been mandated by the School Board to formally address recent developments, not the least of which is the impertinent letter which has been sent to parents(inappropriately using a school letterhead, I should add, as well as school stationery and printing equipment), the extensive memo to the School Board alleging harassment and victimization of staff and students by the school administration, and the very unpleasant experience of seeing the school's good name and reputation tarnished in the daily newspaper.

Please allow me to address briefly several of the matters raised in your letter to parents and the memo to the School Board.

1.Akeem Ali

Akeem Ali was instructed to stand down as captain of the school team. He disobeyed my instruction. Holy Saviour enjoys an undisputed standing as the leading Catholic school in the country. While we accept students of all faiths, it is imperative that the school maintain its reputation as a provider of Catholic education and principles. Ali's selection as captain was therefore untenable in these circumstances.

Fr de Boissiere has an extensive list of disciplinary complaints against him, and reports that he has a very confrontational manner. In addition, he has been observed distributing Muslim pamphlets and propaganda on the school premises, which is clearly intolerable. He was also part of the Student Council that printed and distributed several scurrilous pamphlets attacking the Principal and individual members of the school administration.

2.Victimisation / harassment of students

Certain students always require closer attention and supervision than others. In each of the cases cited in the staff memo, the individuals concerned have all acknowledged the behaviour or infraction of school regulations that necessitated administrative intervention.

3. Victimization / harassment of teachers

Again, it is the function of the school administration to ensure that teachers perform to the best of their abilities, and to assist in relocating those who are clearly deficient into other more suitable occupations. We have had to do so in the cases of Mr Assing, Mr Mahabir and Mr Charles, all of whom were missing classes, failing to complete the assigned syllabuses, had disciplinary issues in their classes or were reported by students as being incompetent in their jobs. There has been resistance from teachers in certain instances, but I have had to stand firm here.

I have also had cause to write to certain teachers on matters of insubordination or aggressive behaviour towards members of the school administration. I was personally ill at ease, for example, when confronted on the staircase by Mrs Harripersad over a matter involving her car, and by Mr Pierre when asked for an apology over his absence from a scheduled staff meeting.

I regret to add that members of the religious community, who live on the school premises, have been often horrified at nights to hear the insulting remarks and crude comments publicly hurled in their direction by clearly intoxicated members of staff returning for their vehicles left on the school compound.

Mr Kalloo was removed as Sports master for failing to ensure that an administrative directive was obeyed. Seeing his signature among those on the memo prompts me to question his maturity and sense of responsibility.

As I have often stressed, in matters of discipline at Holy Saviour, I intend to put my foot down with a heavy hand. I reiterate that if any member of staff honestly believes that a policy of oppression or victimization is being pursued, the only proper course of action for such a person is to leave the staff.

A copy of this memo is being sent to each parent.

Fr Arthur Brady, Principal

22 October

Dear Teaching Staff at St Saviour's

Let's get things in their right perspective. Schools are for studying, character building, equipping one for a livelihood. Sport is a secondary subject, a pleasurable addition to the curriculum.

We the parents take up arms against your laying down yours. Your action of 'no active teaching' is depriving students at Holy Saviour's of your paid services. Your primary concern is in the classroom, furthering the studies of the entire college. Why not leave the entire Ali affair in the capable hands of the relevant authorities?

We see the principle involved as one of loyalty: loyalty to your Principal, to the discipline of the school, and to the pupils and their worried parents. The action you have undertaken could hardly be called the action of a mature, responsible body of teachers.

Please consider your attitude carefully. Students must not be used as a tool for politics, particularly in this island where Government has ensured that free secondary education is for all.

Yours faithfully

Margaret Henry, on behalf of many worried parents.

The Chronicle, 24 October

THEY SHOULD NOT HAVE DONE THIS

Dear Editor

I have received a letter from the teaching staff at Holy Saviour's indicating their intention to 'work-to-rule.' This resort to industrial action is the sort of change for which I was never prepared when I chose Holy Saviour's for my children's schooling.

Many issues are raised by this development. Can any student have the right to challenge a principal's decision? I am certain that the action taken by the administration only occurred after long and careful deliberation.

That the football captain has the support of his fellow students is not surprising, since students welcome any opportunity to challenge those in charge. As for the allegations of victimization and discrimination, this is a wild and general statement that has not been supported by any evidence.

I do hear, however, from many students, that some teachers come to school complete with their graduate qualification but do little more than pass the time on subjects other than what the timetable prescribes.

Rules and regulations, and the discipline as well as authority which the Principal must exercise were fundamental to my choice of Holy Saviour's. Had I not felt strongly about these, I might just as well send them to the Government school around the corner.

Past-Pupil and Present Parent

The Chronicle,24 October

MINISTRY INTERVENES IN COLLEGE CRISIS

(reporting by David Webb)

The Ministry of Education has intervened in the ongoing crisis at Holy Saviour's College.

A School Supervisor III has been appointed to investigate the events that led up to the current work-to-rule at the school, and to report back to the Ministry in seven days.

In the meantime, the Minister of Education has urged teachers and administration to put aside their differences for the sake of the students. 'Many of these students will be writing crucial examinations in just over six months,' says the release signed by the Minister. 'It is in the best interests of all to have this atter resolved amicably in the shortest possible time.'

25 October

Dear Mam and Da

I must confess to becoming very depressed about how things are transpiring at Holy Saviour's.

The matter has escalated dramatically, and there are now stories and letters in the press on a daily basis about the school and what is happening.

The teachers themselves are now divided; some are going back to their classes and teaching; others are holding out and awaiting the outcome of the Ministry of Education's investigation of the matter. Even after it is resolved, I fear that things will not be as they were before. There will be resentment and hostility on all sides, and no clear idea about how this will be healed, if at all.

This is what I gather anyway from the colleagues with whom I shared that wonderful bottle of Bushmills you sent. I did not know before I came that there has been a lot of social unrest in Trinidad over the past few years. People appear angry that they are not getting a fair share of the country's resources, and that their grievances are continually being ignored or downplayed by the government.

Interestingly, I have only now begun to understand a little more about this current unrest in the school as a result of hearing this. My friends told me that that is why the Student Council was dissolved by the Principal last year. He was concerned that the Council was encouraging students to get caught up in these social issues and were printing and distributing pamphlets on things like racism and injustice in the school itself.

I am now beginning to feel just a tad uneasy myself at times when I walk through the streets sometimes. I feel that everyone in the street is looking daggers at me behind my back, although I know that's just my imagination. But I avoid those large meetings in the nearby Square. During a huge street demonstration last week, I remained in the bookshop I was visiting until the excitement was over.

Fr de Boissiere told me privately as well that he thinks the Principal has handled the matter quite badly. He said that he did not show any understanding of the changes happening at the moment in this society. He himself didn't think having a Muslim captain the school team was something he should have made into an issue, and he feels the entire thing now seems to have taken on a slightly racial aspect as well. I don't know, but I often find myself wondering at Fr de B's sincerity in this entire affair.

To make matters worse, I loaned some money, a thousand local dollars, to a fellow who joined the staff at the same time as I did, at the end of September. He said he hadn't been paid for the month yet but would reimburse me as soon as he was. Apparently he also took money from other members of staff as well with the same story. No one has seen him since; it now seems that he was a professional scammer, like some of those we have at home.

How is the weather at home? I'm really beginning to feel homesick for County Cork.

Your loving son, Liam.

12 November

From: SS III Charlene Harris, Ministry of Education

To: Hon Minister of Education

Subject: Disturbance at Holy Saviour College

Please be advised that following on the investigation we have conducted at Holy Saviour College, we wish to make the following recommendations:

1.Mr Akeem Ali, student, must write a formal apology to the school's Principal, and agree to abide by the existing policies of the school. He should be allowed to write his A Level examination in June next year. He should however be debarred from representing the school in any sport, as per the Principal's wishes.

2.Messrs J.Assing, L.Harripersad and A.Charles should be transferred to positions in other schools with effect from the start of the next school year, as soon as equivalent positions are found for them.

3.Mr W. Anderson and Mr Taylor be formally sanctioned via written communication by this Ministry for their roles in this unfortunate affair.

The complete report of our investigation is attached for your review.

C Harris, School Supervisor III

30 November

Mr J Kalloo

Teacher II, Holy Saviour College

Sir

I wish to inform you that the staff report which was submitted on your work and conduct for the previous school year contains the following Box 4 Marking:

(i) 'Does not take his responsibilities seriously'

You are hereby advised to make every effort to overcome this shortcoming in the future.

A des Vignes/ for Permanent Secretary, Ministry of Education.

2 December

Fr A Brady, Principal

Holy Saviour College

Dear Father

I wish to express my regret over the unfortunate incidents of the past few weeks.

I sincerely believed that it was in the interest of team unity and continuity that I disregarded your instruction to step down as captain. Much trouble might have been avoided had there been proper channels for student-staff-administration discussion and relationships. I do agree that all institutions must respect authority for discipline to be maintained; authority should, I am sure you agree, must not appear to be thrown around at the whims and fancies of any individual.

If I have appeared to be overly critical, please accept such as being made in the best interests of the school as an educational institution. You are aware, I am certain, of the growing sense of alienation not only within the school population but within the wider society, where the perception is that certain elements within these bodies do not seem to have the ear of those with authority.

I apologise for any consequences my action may have had on the functioning of the school and confirm that I am willing and prepared to submit myself to college discipline and to obey College rules.

Yours respectfully

Akeem Ali

cc C Harris

SS III, Ministry of Education

3 December

The Permanent Secretary

Ministry of Education

Dear Permanent Secretary

I write in response to a memorandum from your office dated 19 November and signed by Ms C Harris, SS III, in which I have been advised that I shall be transferred out of Holy Saviour College to another school as soon as a position can be found for me elsewhere.

Please be kind enough to note as follows:

1. I have not requested, nor have I agreed to, any such transfer. Teaching Service Regulations do not sanction the arbitrary transfer of any teacher save and except for such teacher having requested or agreed in writing.

2. I have been a member of the staff at Holy Saviour's for nearly twenty years. Over this time, there has never been a single adverse note filed in my annual confidential report to which I have had to respond. The justification for the transfer being envisaged therefore demands explanation.

3. If the request for my transfer has been instigated by a third party, to wit, the Principal of Holy Saviour, he has had neither the foresight nor decency to discuss such with me.

4. I have a home in Port of Spain, and my children attend schools here as well. Dislocation will prove an unnecessary burden on

both my family and me.

Please be advised therefore that I have retained legal counsel in this matter, and that I shall stoutly resist any such attempt to initiate such a transfer.

Yours sincerely

Linda Harripersad, Teacher II

Cc Fr A Brady, Principal, Holy Saviour College

Ms C Harris, SS III, Ministry of Education

FROM THE OFFICE OF THE PRINCIPAL

TO ALL MEMBERS OF STAFF

12 December

I take this opportunity, as the term closes, to wish each and every member of staff a blessed and joyous Christmas. I look forward to welcoming you all back soon in the new year.

I regret the unfortunate events that caused such upset to us all during the school term now ending. I do however have every confidence that all ill-will shall be dispersed, if it has not already, over the Holy Season ahead.

I take this opportunity to say goodbye on behalf of all to Mr Liam Kelly, who has resigned his position and shall be returning to Ireland. We are sorry to see him go but wish him Godspeed.

Fr Arthur Brady, Principal

INSPECTOR PARTAP INVESTIGATES

Inspector Partap twirled the ends of his handlebar moustache as he had seen his favourite television detective do and looked around at the gathered assembly.

At its centre was the disheveled Mrs Scott, newly rescued from being kidnapped, dressed still in the business suit in which she had been snatched two days before. Her husband, Patrick, had a consoling arm around her shoulders; the other hand held a handkerchief which he offered his wife from time to time so that she could dry her eyes and perhaps blow her nose; whenever the latter happened, however, Mr. Scott would take the kerchief back somewhat disdainfully, holding it almost at arm's length, and lay it on the nearby sidetable.

The Scott children, Michael and Anna, sat nearby on armchairs. Michael continued to look intently at his mother; Anna affected an air of some disinterest, as if to say that the matter was now concluded and that they should all go about their respective business. Partap made a mental note and decided that Anna Scott warranted further investigation in the future, perhaps over a rum cocktail in a nearby establishment. Decidedly something chic and genteel, he thought, not the Police Canteen back at headquarters.

Two forlorn looking men, one handcuffed to an extra-large policeman alongside and the other to an athletic-looking corporal, scuffed the carpet on the floor with their shoes as they looked downwards. One of them was rewarded with a severe clout to the head from his corpulent police guardian and stopped immediately; the other policeman seemed to take no notice of his charge's scuffling until the Inspector stared pointedly at him and frowned, at which point he jerked abruptly on the handcuff and brought his prisoner to attention.

'So,' said Inspector Partap grandly, 'these is the men who kidnap you? Nice, nice.' He walked over to each of the two accused and looked them over from head to toe. 'You,' he said to the one nearest, 'What you name?'

'Rohan, sir. But I didn't kidnap nobody, sir, this is…'

Partap put a commanding hand up and he stopped. 'And what is yours?' he suddenly asked the other, whirling around sharply and pointing at the other prisoner.

'Marlon. But as me pardner say, I ent kidnap nobody.'

'Shush. This ent no court. You go get a chance to plead innocent later. Right now I just looking at the evidence. Miss Scott, you sure these is the fellas who kidnap you day before yesterday?'

Mrs. Scott whimpered and shook her head in assent.

'How you so sure?' demanded Inspector Partap. 'We didn't catch them at the scene. We have no evidence tying them to the crime. Is only you say so. What make you so sure?'

'Now look here,' said Mr. Scott, 'you implying that my wife lying?'

'Mr. Scott, I is a police. We have to make sure we not locking up the wrong people. Your wife say is them, but she was blindfolded all the time, so she never see them. She say she recognize they voice, but to me they talking like plenty other fellas I does hear on the street.'

'It's them, I say,' cried Mrs Scott. 'I know those voices. I hear them all the time. These were the men who work…worked in our house last month. Labourers. I hear…heard them every day for a month.'

'Take it easy, Mother dearest,' said Michael soothingly. 'Don't let these people get you upset. Listen, Inspector, you can't be a little more discreet in how you questioning my… er… mother? And why you doing this in front of these men? You can't do this later? Or in the station?'

Inspector Partap walked to the French window and gazed outside as if seeking divine intervention. Then he turned to face the assembly. 'You might not be aware,' he said, 'but most of these crimes have to get solved in the first 48 hours; after that all the clues does start to vanish, and people memory doesn't be so good. Look, the best thing we could do right now is reconstruct the crime. Then we could get a better picture of how things happen and who is who and what is what, okay?'

Helen Scott made sure she chose the most alluring business suit she had in her closet, pale pink with just enough cleavage exposed at the collar. She searched her perfume collection and decided on Organza by Givenchy. It was one Rudolph particularly liked. 'It make you smell like a million dollars,' he would say whenever she breezed into his office as a prelude to lunch at The Hideway and the afternoon tryst in his apartment in Glencoe.

She adjusted her hair, picked up her keys and went down the faux-marble staircase to the kitchen below, where the breakfast table was set up, replete with orange juice, coffee, cereal, bacon, eggs and toast. Patrick was already there, reading his newspaper and sipping his coffee.

'Good morning, darling,' she said putting her handbag and keys down on the sideboard. 'Anything interesting in the news today?'

'My shares in NEL just take a dive,' he said ruefully, taking his glasses off and putting the newspaper down. 'I wonder whether that was a good investment at all. I shoulda leave my money in Republic Money Market. At least there it was earning something, even if was small. You smelling good today, sweetheart.'

'Oh, is the same perfume I does wear every Wednesday,' she said. 'You never remember how I does wear them.'

'To tell you the truth, I can't tell one from the other,' he said. 'You have so much in your closet. Every birthday, every Christmas, is perfume and more perfume. You going to the office today? I thought you had enough staff to look after things here for you. You don't have to go. Stay home today with BabyChunks,' he pleaded.

'I not lucky like some retired people I know,' she smiled. 'Real Estate is a hands-on business, person to person. Besides, them girls in my office will skylark if I not there to watch them.'

'You don't have to work, you know,' he said. 'You have everything you want here. I does give you everything you want. Especially at night, ent?'

'That is true,' she said coyly, kissing him on his bald pate. 'Especially at night. But I need to feel independent too. I don't want people to think I only marry you for your money. I might be late tonight,' she said, putting down her coffee cup and heading to the door. 'Viewing appointment at 6 pm. Don't know how long it will be. Bye. Oops, sorry, Michael,' she said quickly, nearly colliding with her stepson who was just entering. 'See you all later.'

'Bye, Mother dearest,' said Michael coldly as she passed by. 'Have a charming day.' He took coffee from the decanter and sat down at the table with his father.

'She gone to work again,' he said, after a minute. 'That is one hard working woman you have there, Dad. Out early, home late every evening. You not worried about her? It have all these kidnappings going on. The wife of a wealthy man is a prime target for kidnappers. And she don't really be careful, going from one strange man house to another.'

Patrick recognized the sarcastic intent of his son's last remark but said nothing.

'How everybody here looking so happy?' said Anna, waltzing breezily into the room. 'Daddy make another million?'

Patrick looked disapprovingly at his daughter. He didn't mind the tattered jeans, he could even tolerate the frayed T-shirt, but the multi-coloured hair and the ring through her nose bothered him. Apparently, or so Helen told him, she had rings on other places on her body as well. A dragon tattoo was rumoured to run from her left breast down to her vagina, but that he could not believe and chose to block from his mind.

'I was just asking Dad how much longer he intend to put up with Helen's infidelities,' said Michael.

Patrick slammed the newspaper onto the table. 'Enough of this kinda talk!' he shouted. 'What stupidness you saying? Your mother is faithful, faithful. She is the most faithful woman I know. Stop trying to make she into a Jezebel.'

'That is true,' said Michael. 'My mother is a saint. Was a saint. A faithful woman. But you leave she to pick up with this gold-digging woman from nowhere, a real tramp, from what I hear. You leave my mother to die in a apartment alone somewhere...'

'Enough!' shouted Patrick. 'Enough! Stop this talk immediately!'

'Another beautiful day in Paradise,' said Anna, munching on her toast and eggs.

Inspector Partap twirled his moustache again and walked slowly to the first prisoner.

'Your name is Rohan, you say? Where you from?'

'Kelly Village,' mumbled Rohan. 'Look, boss, I not involve in anything. I just work here for a contractor last month.'

'Yes,' said the Inspector, 'and in that time you had chance to study the lady movements whole day, day in, day out.'

'Excuse me, Inspector,' whispered the constable to whom Rohan was manacled. 'If he was here whole day, and the lady was out whole day, he really couldna study she movements that close.'

'What you is, a defence attorney? Listen, when I want your opinion, I'll give it to you, understood?'

The constable retreated. Inspector Partap returned to Rohan.

'So where you was on Wednesday when this kidnapping take place? And Thursday as well?'

'I was home. Me wife was sick and I had was to stay home with she. You could ask she. Both days she was real sick. Throwing up and thing. Look, Chief, my wife still real sick. When all you pick me up, I was just taking she to the hospital. We could finish this quick? I have to rush back.'

'You was home with your wife? That ent no real alibi,' said Inspector Partap. 'Wife does lie for they husband every day in this place whenever they get into trouble. I had a case once where the wife…chut, forget that. Is only your wife could vouch for you?'

'Miss Mohan from next door did bring some soup for lunch on the Wednesday. She see me there. And Thursday I did have was to take she to the doctor. She pregnant, Chief, and she sick real bad.'

Inspector Partap twirled his moustache, then stroked his chin. 'This Miss Mohan, she is your family? No? Hmm… doctor involve. Well, I go have to check out that story. Constable, write down that lady name, Miss Mohan. And get the doctor name and address too; if he have a telephone, call him. We have to check these things thoroughly. And you, what is your story?' He pivoted towards Marlon, the other detainee.

'Boss, this is real stupidness going on here. I was on a job in Princes Town last Wednesday. It have plenty fellas could testify they see me there. It have one call Tall Boy who was even working with me. You could ask he. I don't know why this lady trying to get we lock up.'

'Tall Boy? That ent nobody name. What is this friend real name?'

Marlon looked uneasy. 'The thing is, he not really a friend, he is ...well, he was a co-worker. I only know him that day. Is the contractor hire him. You go have to check the contractor for his real name.'

'Aha,' said Inspector Partap, 'so you don't really know this Tall Boy but you want the police to go around chasing your alibi. Very smart. And what about Thursday? Where you was on Thursday?'

Marlon shuffled his feet and looked down, remaining silent. Inspector Partap sensed an opening. He looked around at the assembly, then turned again to Marlon, stabbing his finger in the air.

'I put it to you that you wasn't nowhere in Princes Town. I put it to you that you and somebody, maybe this Rohan self, kidnap Miss Scott and hold she for ransom on Thursday, but she get away from all you and that spoil everything.'

Corporal Joseph, to whom Marlon was handcuffed, leaned over to Inspector Partap and said something quietly to him. Inspector Partap recoiled in surprise.

'What? What you say? A informer? He is a police informer? How come nobody tell me that? And in a drug inquiry?'

'Yes, you idiot. I is a police informer. And I was helping the police with a drug deal on Thursday. But thanks. Now you tell the world. Now my dogs dead. I ent going to last a week outside now. But some big people going down with this business.' Marlon looked across at the members of the gathered Scott family. 'Some big people!'

Patrick was still upset with his son. The orange juice that he had had at breakfast was curdling in his stomach, and he felt the acid reflux making its way up to his throat. He looked across at Michael, who was calmly eating his breakfast. I have to cut that boy out of my will, he said to himself, then realised he had already done so. He really have no respect for my wife. Even if she is not his real mother, he can't be spreading ugly rumours about she. At least, she wasn't sponging off him for money like he was.

'When you going to get a work, Michael?' he asked across the table. 'You is thirty-five years old. Is high time you start looking to earn for yourself.'

'You must be crazy,' said Michael coolly. 'You want me to give up rent free accommodation in this mansion, all meals included, and get my hands dirty?'

'At least you could start thinking about your future. How long you and your sister planning to live on what your mother leave? That inheritance going to finish soon. What you all going to do then?'

'I don't know about Michael, but I already making plans,' said Anna, putting her coffee down. 'I have big plans.'

'Big plans?' snorted her father. 'Who you think going to hire you when you dress like that and have earrings in your nose and thing?'

'Yes, Anna, what kinda big plans you have?' Michael remarked sarcastically. 'You going to work like Daddy? Build a big construction company with juicy contracts from his pals in the government? You have enough money to make the initial bribe payment?'

'I never bribe nobody!' Patrick exclaimed.

'You never bribe? How you get contracts without even having the equipment and any track record in construction when you start out?'

'I was willing to work hard. I was ambitious. People recognize that. Yes, I had some friends in the right places, but I was always a proven performer.'

'Yes, Mister Ten Percent say so in your retirement function. And now he finish with you, he find another proven performer real quick.'

'I want to be a proven performer too,' chirped Anna. 'But I looking for my own contacts. You have any recommendations, Daddy?'

'Why you didn't pass the business on to me?' asked Michael. 'I coulda continue the construction company same way you did.'

'My company woulda bust in two years with you in charge and I woulda have nothing,' said Patrick. 'I do the best thing. I sell out. I get a good deal. I have a house for me and Helen, I have enough money for us to live out life real comfortable. I not sure how you and Anna going to make out when all you mother inheritance run out, I saying again.'

'So you not leaving anything for us, Daddy?' asked Anna. 'You leaving everything for Helen?'

'That is the plan,' said Patrick. 'I tired tell all you so. I make my way for myself. Both of you had every chance to do the same. Instead, all you waste every opportunity you bet, and now you sitting like corbeaux, waiting for Daddy to dead. But Daddy don't plan to dead just yet. So all you better have a plan B.' He picked up his newspaper and went out onto the patio.

Michael looked at his sister. He wondered at times whether she existed in the real world. She had dropped out of university after one year and followed her rock musician boyfriend at the time over Eastern Europe until he dumped her and returned to his childhood sweetheart. Anna, now devoid of financial support from any source, had no choice but to return to Trinidad and her father's house, where she discovered that her deceased mother had left her a reasonable inheritance which, like his, was approaching its final balances. She would disappear from the house early in the morning, he noticed, and return late at nights; sometimes she would not return until the following day, the scent of marijuana smoked in copious amounts draped about her like the incense from some exotic flower.

'So we definitely going to be disinherited,' he said to her finally. 'What you planning to do?'

'Don't you worry about me,' she said, reaching for her cellphone. 'Like I said earlier, I already making plans. Is you who have to ketch. You don't work, you not qualify in anything, your prospects looking real dim. Anyway, excuse me, I have an important call to make.'

She was right, Michael thought, as she left the room, phone to her ear. I have to do something drastic.

'So, Miss Scott, tell me again about Wednesday when you get kidnap. What happen after you reach to work?' Inspector Partap decided to revisit all the details once again. He wasn't sure, but if these men were telling the truth and had the alibis they claimed, he would be back to ground zero. He couldn't go back to headquarters and tell the Assistant Commissioner that he had not made any progress in a matter involving such high-profile people who were so well connected in government circles.

'Well,' said Helen nervously, still apparently shaken by her ordeal, 'as you say, I reach the office about nine-thirty. We had a short staff meeting, then the agents all leave the office for their appointments, all except Jasmine and Rudolph. They had later appointments...'

'These are sales agents too?' interrupted Inspector Partap.

'Yes. Jasmine working with me about five years now. Rudolph only now start, about three months. Anyway, I leave for my appointment...'

'Where was that?' asked the Inspector. 'And what time was that appointment?'

'My appointment was for two o' clock. In Westmoorings.'

'Two o' clock? And you leave the office twelve o'clock? That was very early.'

'Yes, but I had to stop in Massy stores to make...buy some groceries. I decide to do that before I went to the appointment.'

'Okay. But we didn't find no groceries in your car when we examine it.'

Patrick was annoyed by this comment. 'Inspector,' he said sharply, 'you ever think the kidnappers take the groceries themselves? What you think they must be feed my wife and theyself when they had she? Come on, man, I thought you was the brightest and best on this Anti-Kidnapping Squad.'

Michael laughed, a short cynical laugh when he heard this. Anna took a deep drag on her cigarette.

'I have to ask all the pertinent questions,' said Inspector Partap, 'and I have to ask you please, not to interfere in a police matter. I questioning a witness here. Did you,' he turned again to Helen Scott, 'did you notice anything strange? You know, like people following you, in car or on foot? Anything?'

'Well, I see a van behind me in the rearview, a white van, but I didn't take it on. Is a public road.'

'You notice the number?'

'Like I say, Inspector, I wasn't really noticing these things.'

'And what happen then?'

'Well, suddenly I feel somebody grab me and put a cloth over me face. Then like they shove me into a vehicle, a van, I think. After that, nothing. I was in a blindfold from then until I jump out the car this morning. I don't even know how long they keep me.'

'Two days,' said Inspector Partap. 'They snatch you Wednesday and you get away Friday morning. Two days. They treat you good?'

'Yes, they give me some biscuit and juice and thing. They didn't abuse me if that is what you mean.'

'That was the grocery you make, right? Biscuit and juice. And what make you sure was these two fellas here?' said the Inspector. 'Their voices, you say?'

'Well,' said Helen, 'it sound like them. One was wheezing, like he had asthma. But he had a gruff voice. The other fella didn't talk much, but he had a kinda high-pitch voice, like that one over there. I remember hearing voices like that last month during the renovations. But now I not so sure. Both of them say it wasn't them, they say they was elsewhere. So now I not so sure.'

Inspector Partap turned away. Same damn thing every time, he thought. Every damn witness unreliable. The woman was so sure was these fellas. She tell she husband so when they went and pick her up in Caroni this morning. Now she not sure. And the fellas had alibis, at least one of them, and I sure the other one too. What I going to do now? The ACP bound to bawl me out when we go back to the station. And without these fellas I have nothing. I wonder if the children involved.

'Chief' said Rohan, now very agitated. 'Please. I have to go and see after me wife.'

Michael walked past his sister, who was still speaking in hushed tones over the phone and fell silent momentarily as he passed by. He walked into his father's home office, picked up the phone and dialed.

'Stretch? Meet me in the bar. Half an hour.'

Unlike what his nickname suggested, Stretch was a short, mean-looking individual, a cap pulled low over his left eyebrow and a toothpick sticking out from the side of his mouth. He listened intently as Michael explained his predicament. Stretch recognized immediately that it was his predicament as well. Without the largesse that Michael dispensed so liberally in his direction, Stretch would no longer be able to bestow the gifts on Gloria to which she had become accustomed. Once that happened, it would just be a matter of time before some sweetman swooped in and snatched her away.

'So what you thinking?' he asked Michael. 'You thinking of bumping off your old man?'

'You is an ass or what? Bump him off and she getting everything one time. No, I have to think of something else.'

'Well, why you don't bump she off instead?' Stretch suggested. 'I know some fellas. It would be easy. Ent you say she always driving about by sheself? Them thing easy to arrange these days. And not too expensive. Fellas eager to put down a work these days and is competition for business.'

'That sounding real extreme,' said Michael. 'It must have another way.'

Anna was getting excited over the phone.

'That proposition sounding better by the minute? What is the possible payoff? Three million? And what my cut going to be? Half? One point five million would suit me just fine. When you planning to proceed? Tonight? So soon? I didn't realise it woulda be so soon. No, no, I don't have no problem with that, I just didn't expect it to be so soon. What time by you? Six-thirty? And when...oh, okay, they don't want to telegraph their movements. Okay, I will reach by you for six o' clock and we go wait. And you say you could trust these people? Okay, I will take your word. But remember not to involve me in the business. I will stay out of sight. Yes, I could stay on the porch. Leave some drinks outside, maybe a joint or two. I go be real nervous. Okay, bye. See you later.'

Patrick stared at the letters in his hand in disbelief. And the photographs. The photographs! She had left the key to the drawer in her vanity dresser, probably in her hurry to leave. He had wandered in, seen the key, made to move the key onto the top of the dresser when curiosity drove him to open the drawer. And there, beneath some underwear and other knick knacks, the letters. Wrapped in pink ribbons. Several packs of them. And photographs. He didn't think his wife could be so vulgar. He looked disgustedly at them, and felt the blood rushing to his cheeks, then to his forehead. He opened the first letter on top the pile and read. 'Your darling forever.R.' R...Rudolph. The bitch was horning him with her employee. There were others, he now saw, as he began rifling through the letters. Alan. Bruno. Somebody who signed himself 'Your Tiger.' He felt an uncontrollable rage. He felt a need for revenge. He couldn't wait till she came back. It was time to make some calls, he thought grimly.

'Inspector, I call the doctor. He say yes, the man bring he wife to clinic yesterday,' reported the constable.

'You sure was the doctor you talk to? Where you get the number? He give you? Suppose was some friend he have pretending to be a doctor. Nah, I not convinced. Check the telephone book. All you have a telephone book here?' asked Inspector Partap.

'Oh God, man, me wife could be dying right now. She was bleeding last night.' Rohan was desperate.

'Let the other one go, the informer,' Inspector Partap instructed the corporal. 'If he is a informer, we can't doubt that. He wouldn't be involve in no stupid kidnapping. Let him go. But keep the other one,' he said, turning to the constable, 'until we doublecheck that doctor story. Where that telephone book?'

Patrick retrieved a telephone directory two years old from his office. 'You know they don't print directory anymore,' he said to the Inspector.

'You looking distress,' Inspector Partap said to Helen, who had begun fanning herself with her husband's handkerchief, and was clearly perspiring.

'I okay,' she answered. 'Just a little tired.'

'Perhaps you need a glass of water.' He looked around at the members of the family. For a moment, no one moved. Then Anna got up and walked towards the kitchen.

'Chief, I have to use the bathroom,' said Rohan in an urgent tone. Inspector Partap looked quizzically at Patrick.

'Two doors on your left down the corridor,' said Michael. 'Remember to wash.'

The constable and his charge headed in the direction pointed. Helen Scott continued fanning herself. Corporal Joseph led Marlon to the door, chatting quietly as they walked. Patrick Scott sat silently brooding. Michael Scott thumbed idly through a magazine on the side table. Inspector Partap twirled his moustache.

'You have to leave already?' asked Rudolph, getting up from the bed and putting his arms around Helen, who was applying lipstick.

'Yes, it late, almost seven o' clock. Patrick go start really asking questions now. Lemme go, nah man. Tomorrow, we go come here again, tomorrow.' She looked around. 'I really like this apartment you have,' she said to Rudolph. 'It private, a small compound, one or two neighbours, everybody discreet. Come, gimme a lift to the car.'

'You park in the back of the carpark as usual?'

'Yes. I don't ever park anywhere else. Anybody passing on the main road will see my car in Massy carpark and start asking questions if they see it there too long. Come, let's go.'

She picked up her bag, walked to the door, opened it, then suddenly jumped back into the room. 'Oh shit!' she exclaimed. 'Anna in the balcony opposite!'

'Anna? Your daughter? What she doing there?' Rudolph went to the window, cracked the blinds open and peeped out. 'She see you?'

'I don't know. Maybe. It was dark, but it had lights. I jump back quick, but I don't know. She looking in this direction?'

Rudolph peered through the blinds again. 'It hard to say,' he muttered, 'she talking to somebody on the balcony, but I can't tell if she looking over here.'

Helen began fidgeting nervously with her handbag. 'Oh God, I hope she didn't see was me. If Patrick only find out...' She began pacing about the small room again. 'Look again. See if she watching.'

'No, but she and the fella talking plenty.'

'Who fella? '

'That's the apartment owner. In fact, he own all the apartments in this complex. You ever hear about Mister Big? That is Mister

Big.'

'Mister Big? The drug dealer?'

'The man self. Dangerous man. How your daughter mix up with him?'

'You asking me? How the ass I go know? Shit, this is problems. I can't leave with she on that balcony. You have a back door?'

Rudolph shook his head. 'These apartments don't have no back door. It have a porch in the back, but we is ten stories up. You can't go down from there. Is only the elevator down the corridor there. And the fire escape next to it.'

'Why they design these apartments so stupid?' she hissed. She sat down, got up, sat down again. After fifteen minutes, she asked him to look again. They were still there. At about ten thirty, there was some activity, he reported. Anna had remained on the balcony, but her companion had gone inside. Someone seemed to have arrived. The curtains were drawn. Anna remained outside.

'This is absurd,' she said through gritted teeth. 'What's happening over there? Why she still there? Look, Patrick call my phone about five times already!'

Rudolph turned towards her, a serious look on his face. 'It look like some kinda drug deal going down over there,' he said grimly. 'Your daughter involve in some kinda drug business. You know anything about that?'

'She ain't my daughter,' said Helen angrily. 'That is Patrick child. I not surprise to hear she in drugs. How I going to explain to Patrick how I out so late and not in touch?'

Rudolph thought for a moment. 'You could always say you get kidnap,' he offered finally.

Inspector Partap rushed back into the living room from the

garden, where he had been deep in thought. The constable was in a panic.

'He get away! He get away!' he was shouting. 'He squeeze through the bathroom window and pelt off!'

Corporal Joseph rushed out of the front door, gun in hand.

'How he do that?' demanded Inspector Partap.

'I unlock him so he could take a pee and baps, the man fly through the vent. I never see anybody squeeze through a vent so small yet.'

'You is a real jackass,' said Inspector Partap. They heard Corporal Joseph shouting from outside, then two shots rang out. Inspector Partap rushed to the door and went outside. All the members of the Scott family got to their feet in alarm.

There was a pointed silence. After a while Inspector Partap reappeared at the door.

'Is...is the man okay?' asked Helen Scott, suddenly very apprehensive. 'The corporal shoot him?'

'This is bad, really bad,' muttered Patrick. Michael had turned a whiter shade of pale. Anna suddenly had a moment of revelation and looked closely at Helen as if recognizing someone.

'No,' said Inspector Partap. 'The corporal miss by a mile. He put two hole in somebody car that park outside. The man escape. But we go pick him up later. I think we know how to find him.'

'Is a grey Mercedes he hit?' Michael enquired in alarm. 'A coupe... a sports car?'

'Could be. I not sure. But this case becoming very complicated now.' He looked briefly as Michael ran out of the room to check on his car. 'I would like all of you to come down to the station tomorrow morning at nine o'clock,' he said. 'I think this investigation only just starting. Bullets fire. Now I have to go and file a blasted report. Come, constable, let we get Corporal Joseph. He outside, and not looking too happy.'

As he got to the door, Inspector Partap looked back at the members of the Scott family still inside and seemingly dumbstruck in their seats. He twirled his moustache. They had it easy today, he thought to himself; tomorrow they would find out why his fellow officers called Richard Partap 'The Big Dick'. Anna especially, he hoped.

THE ROAD TO
HAPPY ACRES

'I'm leaving,' she says quietly, holding his hand as they walk to the banks of the stream. It is her favourite neighbourhood spot; she takes him there on afternoons, away from the stifling heat of the houses and the manicured lawns, away from the paved concrete roads and the luxury vehicles parked in every other driveway.

He knows that she is serious; she has already shown him letters from her uncle in Washington, looking forward to seeing her soon. He has been with her to the US Embassy for her visa interview. Still, he cannot accept what he knows to be inevitable. He says nothing.

'So tell me again, why you not coming with me?' she says. 'A man with your intelligence would thrive in America,' she continues. 'They looking for bright people there. My uncle at Howard. He could get you in a postgrad programme, if that's what you want. Besides, what kind of future you going to have here? This is not a place for ambitious and intelligent people. It will wear you down and you wouldn't even realise it. People here living a real ignorant existence. They have no idea of anything happening around them or in the world outside. Damn, I can't even get a decent book to buy in the bookshops; all they have is Mills and Boon, westerns by Louis L'Amour and detective thrillers. My uncle tell me to read a book called The Wretched of the Earth by Frantz Fanon before I come to Washington. I can't find that book anywhere. Not even in the Public Library!'

He hears the exasperation in her voice 'We are really victims of our history,' he finally says. 'If we all leave, what will happen here? More decay, more stagnation. The country would go nowhere. Some of us need to put our hand up and say that we going to try.'

'Patriotism. The last refuge of a scoundrel. That is something you tell me Samuel Johnson write, not so?'

'You quoting him out of context,' he says. 'I just come out of University here. I feel I have to give back a little of what I have been lucky to get. You not feeling the mood in the country? People waking up, challenging the way things are. I want to be part of that, to say that I make a contribution to the cause of building a nation.'

'That's a real pity,' she says. 'You giving up a future that we could have together. Two of us could make it out there. Instead, you only dreaming about improving things here on this island. If you think about it, you could always come back later and give it a shot. Stay now and you will stagnate, like everybody else. Ten years from now you will be saying you shoulda leave with me. But it going to be too late then.'

She stands up. It is the dry season, and the water in the stream has been reduced to a vague trickle darting between exposed rocks.

'This place is an intellectual backwater, run by idiots filling their pockets and laughing at citizens while they doing it. These people have no interest in seeing this country prosper and move ahead. With them in charge, the island go remain small, insignificant and backwards. And the people you staying back to help, the rank and file? They drowning slowly in the mess without even realising it. Progress? Change? A pipe dream. I wish you and your fellow dreamers well. I know these street marches and public demonstrations really exciting you. Soon, all that will just be another episode for the history books. But I leaving. My flight booked. Is really sad you not choosing to come with me.'

They turn and walk back to the cul-de-sac where she has parked the car.

Twilight. The streetlights, widely spaced apart, will soon come on, but he knows that eventually there will be none and he will have only the headlamps of his own vehicle to show him the way. The road snakes through thick undergrowth on each side; already clumps of bushes and trees of varying heights are beginning to assume strange outlines, their detail obscured. He travelled this road before, many years ago, but has forgotten how long and lonely it is. He wants to be careful, but he knows he needs to move forward with some urgency.

There was a handful of villages further back, a few isolated sheds already illuminated by hurricane lanterns inside, but now he passes only the occasional cottage along the way. Every now and then he picks up the startled glance of some villager looking backwards in surprise as he hurries home. He overtakes a cyclist, balancing a crocus bag on the handlebars, the red of the cracked reflector on the rear fender of the bicycle glowing in the headlights. The shadows and silhouettes all around seem to press in ominously on the road as the light rapidly fades.

He had asked for directions from a group of limers sitting on a culvert in the first sizeable village he had passed through. No one really knew the place he was trying to describe. 'Boss, you could try up by the lighthouse,' one of them had finally volunteered, 'but I not so sure. Is a good distance away and the road real twisty.' 'Take you time driving, uncle,' says another. He remembers the lighthouse vaguely and decides to drive until he gets there.

At the end of a hot sultry tropical day, the twilight soon fades entirely, and the diminishing half-light yields to an overwhelming darkness. He is unfamiliar with such darkness. He has heard stories about this part of the island, and the hold that old superstitions and belief in the supernatural still have on the minds of the locals. Jumbies and soucouyants come out at night. The village people stay indoors because they know douens can lure them into mischief. The legends say Papa Bois and

Mama D'lo live in a cave deeply secluded in the forest; once they have you, there is no way back home. Here, near the coast, every small village tells tales of young men bewitched by the beauty of a La Diablesse on the road at night and disappearing forever.

He of course has no time for all this superstitious claptrap. Still, he is startled and has to step on the brake pedal when something darts across the road before him. He catches just the red glint of its eyes in the headlights. A forest cat, perhaps, maybe a small deer. He suddenly remembers the time they visited the fortune-teller's tent at a school Mayfair. 'You will be very happy,' she said. 'I see lots of children. Two boys, I see, one girl.' She looked at them quizzically. 'Perhaps you will live away? I see someone crossing dark water.'

He puts his foot on the gas again and moves forward.

The letters come with some frequency. He recognises them immediately, folded in long airmail envelopes, an unmistakeable ballpoint scrawl tracing out the address, written apparently with the same kind of pen. She must have bought a boxful of these, he thinks after a while, for the colour of the ink remains eternally the same. Even as she travels around the world, Hawaii, Germany, France, the Scandinavian countries, the letters still come in their traditional envelopes. The stamps will change, but the letters, written in longhand on legal size yellow pads, are always chatty, contemplative, critical.

My brother has this great job with an airline, she writes, I get family discount on my tickets. So I travel wherever and whenever I can. She spends a few months in Hawaii, (the place that most reminds her of home). She hooks up with some other expatriates, pursuing one business opportunity or another. She signs up with a government initiative offering counselling services to newly arrived immigrants. I'll be home in a few weeks, she writes after a few years, staying with Auntie Edna. Why don't you come and visit?

He still cannot afford a car on his teacher's salary, so he takes a taxi to meet her.

'No car yet?' she remarks.

'Too expensive,' he replies.

'Cars dirt cheap in the States,' she says. 'I driving a used Camry now. Not the latest model but still a great car. You have your driving licence yet?'

He laughs. It is still embarrassing to remember when she tried to teach him to drive, using her father's car. He had found great difficulty balancing the clutch and the accelerator and switching gears smoothly without a terrific grating noise coming from somewhere below the car. After he climbed the roundabout a third time, she gave up.

'I can't understand how an intelligent man like you can't learn to drive,' she had said in exasperation. 'Everybody should learn to drive before they reach eighteen. It does give you...independence.'

So they walk. It is a pleasant neighbourhood; the lawns are all deep green, and neatly manicured, and the houses lie back from the road.

'Very much like where you grow up,' he says after a while 'Orderly. Quiet. Properly middle-class.'

'You still on that scene?' she says. 'You still bitching about being born into a poor family, and the disadvantages you had along the way? Some people can't help the circumstances into which they born. I was born into a well-to-do family. Not my fault.'

Her mother is the daughter of a prominent family from the south of the island, several of whom are lawyers, doctors, academics. She is a senior civil servant within the Customs and Immigration Department; her father has an equally important position with the Board of Inland Revenue

'But the gap too wide,' he says. 'In this country, over 40 percent of the people live below the poverty line. That not fair. We need some equity in the distribution of wealth, in the provision of services, in health.'

'You tell me that years ago, remember? Like nothing change. But look at yourself. Living proof that people could overcome any difficulties in life. Your ancestors come here late, work as labourers in the fields, save, put their children through school and higher education. They sacrifice plenty along the way. Why others can't do the same? Pull themselves up. What is this dependency syndrome so many of them have? Always gimme gimme, looking for handouts. It does drive me crazy. Then they come to the States, work several jobs without complaining, wear the latest clothes and drive a snazzy car. No old junk for them.'

He stoops and touches a ti-marie plant growing in the sidewalk. 'Look,' he says, watching the leaves recoil and close in self-defence. 'You all have ti-marie plants in the USA?'

'How I would know? What a silly question to ask me. Anyway, I getting married,' she says suddenly. 'A guy I met in Miami. From Haiti.'

'Congratulations. I'm sure you'll be happy together,' he responds. He plucks the ti-marie then lets it fall to the ground.

He comes to a road junction and stops for a few minutes. He has no recollection of this intersection. There are no street signs to help. He decides to continue along what seems to be the main road. He sees a quarter-mile road marker a little further along, so he knows he is still on the main road. He looks briefly at the manila envelope on the passenger seat beside him. Dammit, he thinks, why did she choose to come all the way out here?

He wonders momentarily whether she has told her husband that she was travelling, then remembers that she is now divorced. A few years ago, if he remembers correctly. Good Lord, how the years have flown. He still remembers how he fumbled when he first held her hand in the cinema. He has never forgotten the intoxicating headiness of that first kiss in the incandescent glow of the neighbourhood streetlamp so many years ago.

He pulls up in front of a section of fence that he thinks he recognises. He slows his car to a crawl. Yes, this must be it. There should be a gate somewhere soon.

He is here at last, finally recognising the place from the weather-beaten sign at the gate: Happy Acres. *There is no letter this time. A telephone call, brief, to the point. Coming next Friday for a weekend. Can you meet me at the airport? He is there well before the appointed time and is surprised at her appearance. She has aged significantly. Her hair has turned an ashen white. She has lost weight. She shuffles slowly behind as he leads the way, carrying her small suitcase.*

'Are you all right?' he asks as he waits for her to catch up. 'Looks like you having some difficulty walking.'

'Nothing serious,' she says, 'just a bit tired.' He knows she is not telling the truth but doesn't press the issue.

'Aha, you join the ranks of the prosperous!' she exclaims as they get to his car. 'Nice wheels.'

'Company car,' he replies almost apologetically. 'A perk of the job. I manage a small operation on behalf of an American company involved in the oil and gas business.'

'No more teaching, then. So much for the national cause. Now you serving your own cause, not so? '

'The bills were mounting. I couldn't pay mortgage, alimony and child maintenance on a teaching salary. I was lucky to get this position. Besides, I feel that I've done my bit for the national cause.'

They drive out of the airport and turn towards the city.

'Is early still,' she says. 'I tell Aunt Edna I'll be there about 5 pm. Why we don't take a drive to the beach if that okay with you? I would like to see the beach again.'

He turns the Audi northwards at the next intersection, and they are soon through the foothills and climbing the curved road over the mountains. He tries to remember the last time he had been along this road, a year or two probably. He hasn't had much opportunity; his job is demanding and eats into all of his available time.

'What you doing work wise these days?' he asks politely. 'Still working with immigrants?'

'I get laid off a while ago. Budget cuts. I doing a little courier delivery work for FedEx. Helps to pay the bills. We could stop here for a minute, please?'

He pulls over onto the grass verge. She fumbles her way out of the car, lowers her trousers and squats at the side of the road. He notices she is wearing adult diapers before looking away in embarrassment. He opens both the doors of the car on the passenger side to give her some privacy. When she is finished, she holds on to one of the open doors and pulls herself upright. Neither of them says anything. They get into the car and drive on.

The beach is deserted. It's a working day, so he is not surprised. He helps her out of the car, and she holds on to his arm as they walk through the grass and onto the sand. When she rolls up her jeans to put her foot in the water, he sees that her ankles are swollen. The waves are uncharacteristically gentle and hit the shore with just a moderate roar before the water hisses back searching for its home beyond the breakers. She stands there for a while, taking it in.

'In Miami, the entire beach artificial,' she says. 'They bring sand from somewhere and dump it to create that long stretch.'

'Would you like me to take you to see a doctor?' he asks as they drive back towards the city.

'Don't be crazy. No, no doctor, please, no doctor. I'll be okay after a solid night's sleep by Auntie Edna.'

Auntie Edna calls him in a panic halfway through the morning. She fainted away in the bathroom this morning, and I can't revive her, she says. Would he please come and take her to the doctor?

There used to be fruit trees, he remembers, all along the sides of the driveway leading to the main house, but he sees no sign of them now. There was a gazebo as well, some distance off the main house, but it is too dark for him to see if it is still standing.

He had come here with her many years before. It was a popular weekend retreat at the time. Several people sat at the table that Saturday morning. He had recognised a well-known figure among them, one who would later be hanged for murdering a foreign girl friend who had followed him back from the cold north. To another kind of death, he had thought, reading the story in the newspaper a decade later.

There is a light on inside. Good, she is still awake. He isn't quite sure that she will be happy to see him. She had been quite upset with him earlier for taking her to a doctor. The short wooden staircase up to the front door creaks with each step he takes. The door is open but not locked; he turns the knob and pushes the door open, then remembers he has forgotten the report in his car. When he returns with it, she is standing at the door, waiting for him.

'You take your time to get here,' she says, as he steps onto the front porch. The muffled roar of the sea in the background, in successive crescendos, overwhelms the ongoing chatter of the crickets and frogs in the surrounding darkness whenever it crashes against the rocks below.

'I always love this place, this house. We spend plenty time here, my family and me, when we was all very young. Sitting on the porch here or at the back, listening to the sea after the others went to bed. Sometimes I used to go down the track to the beach below and sit on the rocks. I loved the solitude. It make me feel strangely alive at those moments, in my own company.'

'Talking to God?' he asks.

'God. Ha! God... I was a believer then. My mother make sure of that. She used to shake us awake every Sunday at 5 a.m. so that we could go to Mass at the Mount...Where is God now, now that

I need Him the most? I didn't pay my dues then? Surely I entitled to some minor miracle for all that kneeling and praying.'

He puts the manila envelope he is holding as unobtrusively as possible behind his back, but she notices the movement. 'What you trying so desperately to hide? You have my death sentence? Let me see.'

'Let's look at it later,' he says. 'I don't know what it says, probably nothing critical. Let's just enjoy the evening for a while. Did you eat? I brought you a chicken roti from Hosein's. It must be cold by now, but we can warm it up in the microwave. Shall I do that?'

She laughs. 'You forget where we are? I don't think microwaves reach here yet. No electricity. No running water either, just rainwater. Collected in tanks or otherwise delivered by truck. Progress, no? The progress you desert me for so many years never reach this part of the world. Thank you anyway, but I'm not hungry. I have no appetite these days.'

'Not even for rice and red beans, your favourite?'

'For nothing.'

'I didn't desert you,' he says, then looks around uncomfortably. 'What about a drink? A glass of wine, maybe?'

She laughs again. 'Wine? I thought you was a rum and coke man. Unfortunately, it have no alcohol anywhere around here. You have to bring stuff when you come here. I didn't expect to stay around very long. I just bring essentials.'

'You might miss your flight back tomorrow if you don't go back soon. Your family will be waiting for you to return.'

She laughs a third time. 'My family always happy to see the back of me. I am the contradiction all families fear; related by blood, but not a relative.'

'I told your aunt that you were ill. She was very concerned. I said I would try to get you to come back tonight.'

She laughs, derisively this time, then pauses. 'Let me see the report,' she says eventually.

Dr Gill is a soft-spoken medical professional with a family practice. She had agreed to the emergency visit, and he has passed late in the evening to collect the medical report.

'Are you at liberty to discuss the contents with me?' he asks.

'Professionally I shouldn't,' she answers,' but you have a real crisis on your hands, and I think you need to get your friend into a hospital now. Time is really of the essence here.'

'You do need to tell me, Doctor,' he says quickly. 'She hates going to doctors, especially local doctors. I was only able to get her here because she had fainted and had no choice. If I give her this report without knowing what's in it, she will never disclose her condition to anyone.'

Dr Gill sighs. 'She has a huge ovarian cyst. I cannot tell just from the ultrasound, but it is probably cancerous. In addition, her diabetes numbers are out of control, her electrolytes imbalanced, and she is anaemic as well. Did you observe her swollen feet? She is probably on the verge of renal failure. How did she ever get on to an aeroplane in this condition? Please get her to a hospital right away.'

'I'll try. Tell me, Doctor, what you are describing, would it be ...what you might call a terminal condition?'

Dr Gill demurs. 'I can't say that just based on the few tests I've run, and my lack of knowledge of her medical history. But...'

'But your prognosis isn't favourable,' he persists. *Dr Gill makes no reply, except to say that she is sorry she can offer no more. Get her to a hospital. Outside, in the late evening sunshine, he calls Aunt Edna on his mobile phone.*

'This is terrible,' Aunt Edna says. 'You have to go and get her right away.'

'Get her? Where is she? Isn't she with you?'

'She asked for the keys to the family bungalow on the North Coast. Said she was going there for the weekend and called for a taxi to take her. She never told me she was so ill.

'So,' she says, looking up from the report, 'what does all this mean? You know I was never any good at interpreting charts and numbers and percentages. You're an educated man. Tell me in plain English what this say.'

He stumbles a bit, then slowly repeats as carefully as he can remember what Dr Gill has told him. She stares vacantly into the distance as he speaks.

'So that's it then,' she says after he is done, 'I just marking time. Waiting for the Grim Reaper to come bursting through the door.'

'No, no,' he protests. 'Dr Gill doesn't say so at all. In fact, she wants you to get into a hospital as quickly as you can. Modern medicine is marvellous. You have a more than even chance of getting out of this. We should leave as soon as we can.'

'You are one poor liar,' she says tonelessly. 'But that is what you have always been. You always look for positives, even though reality saying something very different. You use to be a dreamer, always looking to change the world, even though it crumbling around you. That is serious self-deception. Now like you join the rest of the world, but in another kind of self-deception. Don't worry,' she says, as she looks at his crestfallen face, 'I always grudgingly admire that about you, in a strange sort of way. You deceive yourself, but you not conscious that you doing it. Is really a kind of... call it naivete'.

She goes to her handbag and takes out two folded sheets. Some items fall to the floor; he moves to get them but she picks them up quickly before he has a chance to help her and stuffs them into her handbag. 'This is my own report,' she says, brandishing the sheets of paper, 'from a specialist in Miami. They don't bullshit you up there. I know my time short.'

He looks at what she hands him. 'You knew this all along? Is that why you didn't want to see a doctor here? Or go to the hospital?'

She laughs mirthlessly. 'You forget ten years ago my father went into a hospital here for minor surgery.' She raises her voice. 'For minor surgery! He was dead in 48 hours. Now you want local doctors and local hospitals to work miracles for me? Don't worry, my friend,' she says, seeing the look of concern on his face. 'Que sera, sera.'

They go to the verandah at the rear. In daylight it commands a majestic view of the Atlantic, and a cool, invigorating trade wind always sweeps briskly through then disappears into the forest. They can see nothing now however save for the dark expanse before them, and the twinkle of endless stars. The sound of breaking waves is unmistakeable; the wind ignores the lateness of the hour and continues to rush past at intervals.

'You know,' she says after a long silence, 'you don't talk much, but you listen well. That is what I always needed in my life, and you have always been there to listen. God, how I miss not having you around when I went away. I miss that listening ear.' She raises her hand and wipes a stray tear from her eyes.

'I travel all over the world,' she continues. 'I live in many different places. But I was always a stranger in a strange land. So here I am, back where I start from. Here. With you. On this island. In a house called Happy Acres in the middle of nowhere. To this place which I try so hard to put behind me yet is still the only place I could call home' She holds his hand. 'Strange, eh? The certainty of your final moments leading you back to the people and places that always matter the most, even though you never acknowledge it.'

They sit there for a while in silence, looking out into the large dark expanse beyond.

'So, are you coming back with me, then?' he asks.

'I'd really like to stay here just a bit longer,' she finally says. 'It's too late now anyway. I'll be ready to leave before morning.' He agrees.

'Isn't there a lighthouse around here somewhere?' he asks, remembering.

'Yes, there is…was…is. It was operated by generator. One day the generator run out of gas. There wasn't any money to buy more. Then the custodian leave. So now we have a lighthouse. But no light. That's the story Auntie Edna told me, anyway.'

'The stars are out tonight. But no moon,' he observes. 'No moon. Only stars. And somewhere a lighthouse without gas.'

'Like a van Gogh painting,' she says.

After a while, he excuses himself. It's been a long and tiring day, he says, and asks if he can crash for an hour or two on the sofa. 'I'd like to make a really early start if that's okay with you.'

She nods and smiles weakly at him and says that she will stay out just a bit longer. 'I need to contemplate my future,' she says. As he turns to go inside, she holds him lightly by the wrist.

'You could turn the lamp off when you go in, please? Thanks.' She pauses.

'And thank you for everything. Thank you for being the best friend I ever had.'

He smiles, puts a hand on her shoulder then goes inside.

Had he known, he tells himself the following day, after the police and the medical examiner and the ambulance and the curious villagers have come and gone, had he known, he would have stayed with her until dawn.

THE MARK OF CANE

I

The first time I saw Lalchan, he was standing outside the Government Railway Station on South Quay looking like he was lost. He was really lost, when you think about it. His father had put him on the train at Rio Claro, pushed a small bag of clothes in his hand and told him not to get off the train till he got to Port of Spain. If he didn't see me, he was to stand and wait until I found him.

It wasn't difficult for me to find him. He stood out like a sore thumb, dressed in a tattered shirt and an oversized pair of brown trousers, a hand me down from some older relative, held in place with a length of twine. I was almost ashamed to go up to him, but I had been sent a message asking me to meet him and help him out and I could not refuse. Blood is an important thing; you have to obey your parents when they ask you to do something, even if you don't like it. Otherwise, you're going to go through this cycle again, and who knows how things will turn out then.

I thought they could at least have gotten him some better clothes for travelling. As it was, everybody on the street looked at us as we walked down Broadway to catch the tramcar going towards St James. I was embarrassed, so the first thing I did was take him into Salvatori and Scott on Frederick Street. I had to drag him off the street, because he was dawdling.

'You have any money?' I asked him.

'Yes,' he said, 'I get a few shilling from me Pa. It have real car in town, gyul. I never see so much car before. In Barrackpore is only donkey cart and bicycle.'

I need to explain that what and how he spoke was almost unintelligible and came over in a country accent as thick as molasses. What I have to do, therefore, is try to reproduce what he said, especially in those early days, in the best approximation of English I can write in the hope that you will be able to decipher it. I was fortunate; although I had lived in St James since I was seven, I was still able to understand when he spoke because that is how my own parents and relatives still spoke whenever I travelled to Caroni to see them, and I remained familiar with the dialect of the village and the fields.

'We have to buy you some proper clothes,' I said.

'Somet'ing wrong with dese?' he said, looking at his reflection in a store window. 'Is dese I does wear when we having prayers.'

'These,' I said. 'These.'

'Eh?'

'The word is pronounced THESE, not DESE. And because you are now in town, you have to dress differently and speak differently and behave differently.'

'Like how you does talk?' he said. 'I find you talking real funny. And you ain't dress like girls in the country. Down by we, gyul does wear simple thing, and have veil on they head, and nice sari when they dress up. You not wearing dem t'ing, you dressing strange. You don't even have a nose ring or nutting.'

I sighed. I hoped I didn't have to put up with him for too long. 'Look,' I said, 'they send... sorry, sent you to town to get a job, they tell me, to help out things at home. Things are very difficult now. To get a job in town, you have to dress properly and speak in a way that people can understand you. So please listen to what I say, okay? Look through this catalogue and see if you can find a shirt, pants and belt to fit you.'

'You does read too?' He was genuinely bewildered.

'And socks and shoes,' I added. 'You cannot walk around Port of Spain in wooden sapats.'

I find that men adjust to changes around them a little more easily than women do. I know I had great difficulty getting used to life in the city when I left for my aunt's tiny bungalow in St James so many years ago. I was seven and cried a lot on the train ride. Aunt Jasodra tried to comfort me a bit but gave up after a while. I didn't like St James. It was muddy, filthy and smelly; I had expected more, like the nicer houses I had seen in Woodbrook as we passed through. I complained to Aunt Jasodra.

'You just have to get accustom!' she snapped. 'What you was expecting, Buckingham Palace? Was sugar estate here too, not long gone. I have no time to hold anybody hand, besides; I have work to do.

She did, in fact. She ran a small vegetable and provision shop on the main road in St James, going for produce early Thursday morning in the big market on George Street and paying a cart driver sixpence to bring her and her shopping back to St James. Lots of Indian families lived in St James at the time, but there was no space in their small lots to plant crops. They kept their cattle on the open public pasture, so her little shop thrived, and she was able to improve her own little dwelling and add an extra bedroom, which is the one I occupied when I came to town.

Aunt Jasodra wasn't a bad lady, but she really had little time for me. She had never married. I remembered my mother alluding vaguely to her having been jilted by some suitor, but I never asked her about it and she never volunteered any information. She expected me to help out around the house, keep my room tidy and be her shop assistant on Saturday mornings when the shop was busy. Otherwise, I was left to my own devices. My father sent money up every now and then to help with my upkeep, and I might get a few pennies for myself, but by and large I was expected to go to school, learn well and get a decent-paying job in some department store or office in Port of Spain afterwards if I was fortunate.

That was how Teacher Kanhai at the Mission School in the village near Endeavour had advised my parents.

'You must send the child to a school in town,' he told them. 'She bright. She too bright to waste she life doing canefield work here in Caroni. Townside they doing well; cocoa making money for them. If she educate sheself properly, she will get a nice work up they. If you don't do that, she go end up making baby here in Caroni and doing nothing with she brains.'

My father was far more receptive to the idea than my mother was. He was probably thinking he would be saving have to find a dowry for yet another of his girl children I thought. My mother required more persuading, but my father took her aside and spoke quietly to her. She yielded only when Aunt Jasodra, Teacher Kanhai's s sister, turned up to take me with her, although my father still had to insist strongly, I judged, hearing them argue in fierce but subdued tones at the back of the house.

'Leh she take she and go den,' my mother finally exclaimed angrily, 'leh she take she and go!'

Thereafter, on the very few occasions that I came to visit, I found my mother strangely distant. Perhaps, I imagined, she still felt hurt and angry over the entire episode.

Aunt Jasodra thought that I might have been badly behaved and difficult to deal with, but I wasn't. She was also concerned about how I would adjust to life in this strange place, and to the classmates of all kinds I would meet in McShine's Primary School in Woodbrook where she had enrolled me.

'Do your schoolwork,' she told me. 'Study hard. But don't mix with other people, especially dem black people children. When you carry you roti and baigan choka or whatever, hide with your paper bag in a corner and eat it dey. Don't take nothing from nobody. These people unclean. Don't go in dey house. Talk to dem, play with dem children at school because you must play. But don't make friends with dem. That is how I survive, me alone, all these years; that is you mus' protect yourself. Everybody dis side 'gainst we. Stick with your own, otherwise, all fall down.'

But when I started doing well in tests at school, she began boasting about me to her customers. I was a little embarrassed at times when she spoke so glowingly of my academic achievements, but secretly enjoyed being lauded this way. She put me in charge of her accounts after a while, keeping track of which customers were trustworthy and those who weren't, getting settlement for outstanding debts and keeping a running total of how she was spending her money and how much she was saving. By the time I was twelve, I did most of the selling on Saturdays as she sat on a stool in the corner and watched.

II

'So how it is you come to read and write English so good?' Lalchan asked me boldly, dropping by after work one evening.

He was fortunate. He had gotten a job with a small construction company that specialised in building houses for the people who had begun to move into the area. St James had been taken over the year he arrived by the Port of Spain City Council, and the drainage and sidewalks were being improved. They were even beginning to name streets after places in India. Our street, 'Bluewater Alley,' now caried the proud name of Lucknow Street. Residences were being built, and even an unskilled worker like

Lalchan found employment fairly easily. The job paid him well enough to afford a small space in someone else's home not far away, and to begin to acquire a decent wardrobe. He now had shirts and trousers that made him look respectable. Aunt Jasodra was most relieved. She had not relished the idea of some distant unrelated family relative she didn't know arriving with little advance notice on her doorstep and was even more keen not to have him sleeping on her sofa for longer than was necessary.

'Well,' I told him, 'when I came to town, I went to McShine's Primary School in Woodbrook. I learnt History, Geography, Mathematics, and General Knowledge, along with English. I had to read books, lots of books, books by people like Charles Dickens and Jane Austen, important English writers.'

'Mathematics? What that is?'

'It's like, er, it's like Arithmetic, just a little more complicated.'

'Hmm! So you could do big sums. I could add and take away, and I know my ABC's, that is all. What more you need than that? But I don't see no Indian man marrying you easy so. No Indian man want wife smarter than he. Dey wouldn't want wife working in office, for sure. But you lucky. The Indian fellas dem I see round here, hmm, best you did marry me,' he said.

He was right. I was not impressed by the neighbourhood bachelors. Most were also too intimidated by Aunt Jasodra to even dare make an approach. When any tried talking to me in the shop, she would get up off her stool and chase him away. 'Gwan from here, you damn Madrasi! Get about your business!'

'Tell me more about dis reading and writing,' Lalchan told me one day. 'Sometimes I does get instruction on paper and does have to ask somebody to tell me what it say. And I could never tell if the foreman cheating me with the wages or not. Dey have everything write down on paper.'

'Well, I suggest you begin by going to school...'

'What?!! You crazy? You and me is nearly the same age! You want to put me in class with children? I ain't no duncey head, you hear? You know how stupid I go look?'

I had to be patient, I realised. 'Miss Boyce in Woodbrook knows someone who could give you private lessons,' I said. 'After work. One or two hours. You will be a top reader in no time.'

One must always give Jack his jacket. Lalchan went to private lessons religiously for almost a year, by the end of which he was able to read most of the newspapers, asking for explanations of certain words so frequently that I bought him a dictionary and showed him how to use it. He followed events when war eventually broke out later in the year, knowing enough to give me a regular commentary how poorly the Allies were doing, and to confirm that the foreman wasn't short paying him every week. But I was never able to persuade him to read Walter Scott or Charles Dickens, far less Jane Austen. He had no intention of reading no book written by no woman, he announced proudly. He did show some interest in the Biggles books that were becoming popular at the time; I often saw him looking interestedly at the dust jackets whenever we went to the library to read the newspapers. But he baulked at the idea of tackling anything that daunting in length.

'Besides,' he argued, 'that Captain Johns only writing about a longtime war. It have real war going on now; why he don't write about dat war instead?'

'If is not one t'ing, is another,' sighed Aunt Jasodra. 'Firs' is protest and riot all over the country, now is war all round de worl'. Lucky for dem dey put dat man Butler in jail. W'en time come, is to send he back Grenada whey he come from!' She had been worried that my father and her brother might have gotten caught up in the unrest that had bubbled over in the sugar and oil belts a year or two before.

Good fortune seemed to favour Lalchan. The Americans arrived in the country and were setting up facilities on Wrightson Road, not too far away, and were happy to get cheap unskilled labour at what they considered bargain prices. He was quickly hired, at a good rate given his construction experience. We began seeing Americans everywhere, even in St James, getting into brawls with the locals or among themselves at times. Lalchan moved to Woodbrook, to be closer to his job, I assumed. I visited him once in the small annex on Alberto Street. I commented on how nicely he had begun to furnish his quarters: a set of Morris chairs, a small dining table with two chairs, even an icebox and a radio. He also showed me the suit and tie he had acquired, which he kept neatly pressed on hangers in his closet.

'You're getting ahead in life, I see,' I remarked.

'You want some Coca -Cola?' he offered. 'The Yankees does get so much, they does give me a bottle or two every now and den. I have a few good soldier friends, you know, sister. Dey real different, dese Americans, very friendly.'

'THESE Americans,' I said. He looked at me quizzically then laughed.

I didn't refuse the drink. Coca-Cola was new to us, and difficult to come by sometimes. I had a glass, we chit-chatted briefly then I left.

III

I got a job with an American company myself, one that did business with the oilfields in southern Trinidad but maintained a small office in downtown Port of Spain. The managing director was fairly blunt and straightforward when he hired me.

'Look,' he said,' I don't mind hiring local but I'm not hiring any Negro people. They're lazy, don't turn up for work sometimes, and their work is often sloppy. It's the same back in the States. I find Indian people over here more professional and harder working. It's difficult to get good ones here in Port of Spain, though, so when Mrs Sylvester told me about you, I told her send you right away.'

I was somewhat taken aback at what he said but pretended to be indifferent. 'Mrs Sylvester was very kind to recommend me,' I answered.

'Yes,' he said, walking to and fro. 'She said you read and write English well, know some accounts, and have shorthand and typewriting certificates. You didn't belong in a department store. Your gifts were being wasted there; you deserved something better.'

'I must thank her again,' I replied, and retrieved my Pitman's certificates from my bag. He looked at them cursorily then handed them back. 'That's fine,' he said. Then he looked at me more closely. 'She didn't say you were an attractive young lady as well. And you dress nicely, too.'

I blushed. I had been whistled at and propositioned on the street several times, but no one had ever said anything complimentary to my face.

Aunt Jasodra was happy to hear the news. 'I glad for you, child,' she said, 'you is over twenty years and is about time you did get a good job. I go send message for you father; he go be glad to hear. Work with dem white people long as you could, you hear. Dey does treat you good. Next thing, you might get marry and go America,' she added, whether in jest I couldn't tell. 'I not feeling to carry on this shop business much longer. It getting too big, and now you gone, I have outsider helping me now, and I nah like dat too much. Them does t'ief from me every day. Next few years I think I done, maybe. I tired. But I didn't want close down de shop 'til you settle a good job somewhere.'

My mother died a few years into the war. She no longer seemed cross with me as she lay on the bier, awaiting cremation. I thought my father looked much older than his sixty years. I asked him if he was feeling well.

'I good, daughter, only a little sad and tired. Everybody leaving me these days. First was your sisters get married and gone with husband. Den you gone. Now your Ma leave me.'

He looked at the canefields that stretched out to the horizon beyond the cremation site. I saw a distant look in his face. 'I always say one day I going back India, to me father village.' He looked sadly at me. 'Over here, cane does put a mark on you, you know, beti. You could try scrub it off, hide it with talk, the cane does hold on and don't leggo. Is like it say you nah leaving dis place. Sometimes you t'ink you escape by going 'way townside or someway, but people seeing dat mark all the time. Is a brand Indian people have on dey forehead. And it have no going back for we either. Cane burying all ah we here, just like it burying me slow, slow. People like we, no escaping cane.'

He let the dirt in his hand trickle slowly to the ground.

'Jasodra say you doing good. Dat nice. How dat boy going?' he asked. 'Your mother relative… what he name again? Lalchan. How he going? He ever tell you he father was in some jhanjat down in Concordia?'

He didn't wait for an answer but walked over to speak to Aunt Jasodra who was sitting in a corner.

I mentioned what my father had said about cane burying and marking you to Aunt Jasodra in the railway carriage as we were travelled back to town. 'What do you think he meant?' I asked her. 'He looked very sad.'

She scratched her head. 'Can't say for sure,' she finally answered. 'Maybe he saying Indian people navel string bury in de canefield. Dat is why dey bring we here from India, you know, and dat is why we remain in the canefield by weself for so long. Dey want we remain dere, too. People here only know we as cane worker and labourer. It don't have much Indian people in Port of Spain, only St James; dem you see, ent is pull dey pulling cart, cleaning street or begging on the road? We is coolie, they say. We does do devil worship and cause trouble. We is not to be 'round dem, but stay far'

She pulled her ohrni tighter around her head.

IV

Aunt Jasodra's worldview began to bother me after a while. Working downtown, and in an office with foreigners, I recognized that she was holding on to a way of life that might have isolated and protected her at one time, but that she was limiting herself from keeping pace with the changing times. Worse, she continued to try to confine me within it as well. I would try to speak to her about the different people I was meeting, all shades and colours of people, and how nice most of them were. She continued to maintain that the world was against Indian people, and that most men were only looking to prey on innocent girls like myself. Still, I was living in her house, and chose not to upset her by open disagreement. I busied myself with work, which became more and more demanding as time went by. I was exhausted on weekends, and only had enough energy to read my beloved classics or go to see the moving pictures in a nearby cinema.

'You'll be an old maid just now,' my boss teased me every now and again. 'No Indian prince come calling yet?'

One or two of the young men who came occasionally to the office offered to take me out at times, but I turned them down, fearing what Aunt Jasodra might say. Instead, she and I went to the movies off and on, to the London Electric and even to the grand new Metro or Empire downtown on St Vincent Street. Sometimes we would ride the tram around the Savannah or walk around the city looking at all the new buildings that were springing up everywhere. Lalchan escorted us once or twice; he seemed to have become popular in the city, for many people hailed him out by name as they passed; he might have offered to introduce one or two had Aunt Jasodra not continued to train her beady eyes on all men in my vicinity, old and young. She particularly disliked the coloured men dressed in dapper suits and two-toned shoes who walked with ladies on their arms on Sunday afternoons around the Savannah

'Don't trust them,' she said, sometimes with a hint of bitterness I found difficult to fathom.'Nah good, dem only cosquel,' she would say, 'Dem so make woman life hard, very hard.'

The war continued to rage abroad. Everyone had ration cards, and people had to line up for everything. Aunt Jasodra finally sold her shop; the prime location had attracted much interest as St James grew, becoming an important transit point for those who lived or worked on the American base on the Chaguaramas peninsula, and she finally yielded to what at that time was a very generous offer. I persuaded her to place the proceeds with a bank that had set up a branch in the area to capitalize on the money that the Americans had been spreading around so generously. She was a reluctant client but trusted me to ensure that the bank was not creaming off her money.

Lalchan came by late one evening. He was wearing a new suit, not the one I had glimpsed in his cupboard a year or two earlier. He told me he had joined up with somebody in Woodbrook who was providing entertainment for the American soldiers, so he no longer had to work long and backbreaking hours on construction projects. I secretly admired his drive and ambition.

'Lalchan? Is you?' exclaimed Aunt Jasodra, getting up from the rocking chair on the porch and peering closely at him. 'Is where you get that nice suit? And look, you have moustache and thing. Beti, come and see this. Is like Sunday morning service out here, girl.'

'Is she self tell me years ago I have to dress better to live in town, not so, sister? Good night, Auntie. How all you doing? I just come by to say hello. I have a little something for all you too.'

I looked at him a little closer in the light. He was certainly sharply dressed, and the moustache he had cultivated gave him a rather dashing appearance. His English had certainly improved, even though I picked up an American twang in his diction.

'You look like Tyrone Power in Mark of Zorro,' I told him. He smiled, a big toothy smile.

He put the tabletop radio he had brought on the dining table. 'This is shortwave,' he said, plugging it in and twiddling with the knobs. 'Look, you could hear radio station from all over the world. America, England, anywhere. Is news and music, BBC, Voice of America, whatever.'

'That real nice, 'exclaimed Aunt Jasodra, 'real nice. How does you find them station?'

'Well, you have to press these knobs and then turn this one to tune in. This other knob is for volume.'

'That is really nice, Lalchan,' I said. 'Thank you. We have one in the office but I don't interfere with it. The new girl the boss hired, she seems to know all about it. She is the one who chooses what station to play every day. She likes WVVDI.'

'It have any Indian station?' asked Aunt Jasodra. 'It only have Indian music on de radio early in de morning or late evening. Whey you get dis, Lalchan?'

'One of them soldier boys getting transfer tell me to take it. He heading to England. Maybe they finally going to invade Europe, who know?'

'Oh, oh,' said Aunt Jasodra, 'so just now no more construction work?'

'Auntie, I leave that work long time. I working with The Rajah is a year or more now. You know, sister,' he said, turning to me, 'he was living just round the corner from me when you come to see me. I shoulda take you to see him.'

'De Rajah?' said Aunt Jasodra. 'Boysie Singh?'

'Yes,' said Lalchan. 'He have one or two club where the soldier boys them does go and drink and play cards.'

'Boysie Singh, you say?' Aunt Jasodra exclaimed indignantly. 'Don't ever dare take dis chile near him or any club he have, you hear me? Dat man is a criminal. Dem club you talking 'bout, is gambling and brothel de man running. He making Indian people shame! Dat is what you come to town to find yourself in, Lalchan? Shame on you! Look, take back dis damn radio wit' you. I don't want nutting connected with dat man in dis house, you hear me? Nobody and nutting!!' She stomped angrily to her bedroom.

Lalchan stood perplexed.

'You better take the radio with you, Lalchan,' I told him. He said nothing but put the radio under his arm.

'That old lady still stifling you,' he said as he left. 'You and me, we go keep in touch.'

I saw little of Lalchan for a few years afterwards. Even when the war ended, he didn't come around, but every now and then, someone would deliver something to the office, a bar or two of chocolates, perhaps, or a tin of biscuits, or butter and cheese, also in tins. The girls in the office all wondered who my secret admirer could be. There was never a card, but I knew who they were from; I had to carry them surreptitiously into the house at times, and if Aunt Jasodra saw or suspected anything, she remained quiet.

V

I followed the stories about Boysie Singh in the newspapers, hoping never to see Lalchan's name mentioned. There were stories about murders being committed, or fights at clubs in Port of Spain, even stories about people trying to get to Venezuela by boat and disappearing forever, but it was all innuendo; no stories implicated Boysie by name, until one day I saw that he was going to be put on trial for the murder of somebody they called Bumper. There were three trials, and it all went on for a long time, but in the end, they freed Boysie. They said he had bribed and threatened the judges. I saw Lalchan's picture in the newspapers one day, among those near to Boysie when he was finally released

Aunt Jasodra died suddenly one night. She didn't come out of her room in the morning, and when I went in, I found her pale and already growing cold. I sent a message for her brother Teacher Kanhai. He telephoned back saying that he was not coming for the cremation, but he eventually did. He told me he was also not interested in having any of her belongings or her house, and that I could keep everything. He was preparing for his final days as well, he said, and had no interest in material possessions anymore. My father came with him but stood drawn and motionless for the entire ceremony. He did not stay after the ceremony. Lalchan had turned up briefly at the cremation site as well, but only nodded to me from a distance and left very quickly, looking nervously about him, which I found very strange.

No other relative came out of the woodwork to challenge for possession, so I inherited the house by default. I simply continued to pay the land rent and whatever bills came to the house. She had left some money in the bank, which she had finally learned to trust, only because I was the person who controlled the account. There wasn't much left in it after I paid for her cremation expenses, but I left it there anyway, just in case, and forgot about it after a while.

My father died later in the same year as Aunt Jasodra. When I went to Caroni for his cremation, I asked one of my sisters what had happened.

'Nothing,' she answered, 'he just waste away. He use to stay in the house and sit on the porch looking at canefield all the time, not doing nothing. He use to go by people house when it had prayers, but that was it. A pundit use to pass by every now and again to read from the holy books. That was it. Seventy years… he live a good life.'

'None of you thought of taking him in?' I asked.

'He didn't want that, he say. He prefer to stay by heself. I come alone, he use to say, and I going alone.'

I recognized the phrase. He had said it to me once before, after Ma's funeral.

'I hear,' whispered my sister, as we watch the flames on my father's pyre leap and dance in the encroaching dark, 'I hear is he who turn down Aunt Jasodra for we mother years ago. That is why Aunt Jasodra leave Caroni and went to live in Port of Spain.'

'Country people really have nothing to gossip about,' I retorted. 'If people have secrets, let them take their secrets to the afterlife with them.'

I said goodbye and went back to St James.

Late one evening shortly afterwards, Lalchan came to the gate and called out. 'Sister,' he said, almost whispering, 'I want you do something for me. I want you call the fella you know does drive taxi and ask him if he could make a drive to Cedros.'

'At this hour?' I asked him. 'Why you going Cedros at this hour?'

'I have to take a passage. I going Venezuela, but don't tell nobody.'

'Venezuela? But why? Why you leaving the country? And so suddenly?'

'Is a long story,' he said. 'Something catch up with me. Is a kinda country thing. I can't tell you details, but I really have to get out the country for a while.'

'Your boss can't help you? Boysie, I mean. He is a man with connections, not so?'

'Nah,' said Lalchan, 'he turn preacher these days. He stop taking people Venezuela.'

He turned and called out to someone I hadn't noticed standing next to a telephone pole nearby. A young lady stepped forward. She was quite nice looking, I remember, lovely copper-coloured skin and hair that had been straightened.

'This is me wife, Patsy,' he said. 'We get marry this morning.'

I was very confused but managed to blurt out my congratulations to the newlyweds. 'But you still not saying why you in such a hurry. No little marriage celebration even?'

'Patsy parents not happy.'

'Why?' I asked.

'They didn't want she to marry no Indian,' he said simply, and left it at that. I went to the telephone and called Mr Jacob. He came over in his huge American car about fifteen minutes later.

'Cedros? So far? At this hour? That will cost you a raise, young fellow,' he said. 'This is all your luggage?'

Lalchan drew me aside. 'Don't go by my house, okay? Stay away. Avoid the street if you could. Leave everything alone,' he said quietly. 'I will send you a postcard from Venezuela. When things settle down.'

He never sent that postcard, and I never saw Lalchan after that. A week or so, a man came to my gate, asking for him. I told him I didn't know where he was, and that he didn't live here. The man looked skeptically at me but left anyway. For a week or two, I thought I saw him hanging around in the St James area, but after a while I had no sense that he was anywhere around.

VI

I continued to work with the Americans in the office. The premises expanded, new employees were hired, different managers came and went, but they kept me on, for continuity, I suppose. Oil had become more important in Trinidad's economy, and big companies like Texaco and Shell were expanding their operations at a rate. I got offers from one or two of them but preferred to stay where I was. I read that Boysie Singh had been arrested for murder again. This time they hanged him.

St James began to change a bit as well. There were more small businesses on the main road; another roti stall appeared on the sidewalk at night. The streets hummed with activity, even after seven or eight o'clock when I walked home from the movies. I enjoyed going to the movies now; the St James Theatre occasionally showed American dramas like Always In My Heart and To Each His Own, but I preferred going to the Roxy whenever they carried the British films like Great Expectations and Oliver Twist. Sometimes, walking home, I was tempted to buy a vegetable roti from one of the sidewalk vendors, but I would hear Aunt Jasodra in my head repeating her warnings about buying food from strangers. Lalchan would have encouraged me, I thought wryly, now that my Aunt was dead.

A few years later, a letter came from the bank, saying that the funds that Aunt Jasodra had left to pay for the security box she had rented there had expired, and would I come to either replenish the account or clear out the box. I went to the bank and emptied the box; there wasn't much in it, some gold bracelets, a necklace and a sealed manila envelope. I put everything in my handbag and went to work, forgetting about them until after supper that night.

I looked at the bracelets, bera, the gold bracelets that Indian women wore on their wrists. The necklace boasted fine filigree work, the kind that I remembered Indian jewellers in Caroni creating in painstaking fashion. I opened the envelope. There was a photograph inside; it was an old one, on which the black and white image had faded to an unattractive ochre, but I still recognized my father, albeit a youthful version. There was another folded document, itself turning brown; it was a birth certificate. I looked and saw my name under 'Child's Name', and my date of birth. My heart raced; I looked under 'Mother's Name 'and saw 'Jasodra Kanhai'. The entry under 'Father's Name' was blank, and the word 'Illegitimate' written in careful copperplate in another column.

I spent a long time in that rocking chair on the porch, looking at that birth certificate. Then I put it back in the envelope with the photograph and placed everything into an old shoebox on a shelf in my cupboard.

About fifteen years ago, a young man appeared at my gate. Even without my glasses, I knew who he was right away.

'Good morning,' he said, politely,'thees be your house, senora?

'THIS,' I said automatically, 'not THEES.'

He looked puzzled. I opened the gate and let him in.

'I am Ramon,' he said, in heavily accented English, 'my father he always say I come look for the lady who live thees house.' He showed me a piece of paper on which my name and address had been written. 'She my sister, he say. She help you find your way.'

'What is your father's name?' I asked, more out of politeness than anything else.

'Oh, his name Lalchan. He from Trinidad, he say, he my mother both, both come Venezuela from Trinidad, hace muchos anos, how you say, long time ago?'

'How are your parents?' I asked.

He appeared puzzled.

'Papa? Mama?' I said, 'they well?'

'Ah, okay,' he said, his face brightening as he understood. 'Mama, she okay, live Valencia. Papa, muerto unos meses, he die two, three month now. Golpe del corazon…what you say, heart?'

'Heart attack,' I said quietly.

'Si, si, heart attack. Very sad time our family.'

The news also saddened me in a way I had not expected. I suddenly remembered him standing outside the Railway Station, looking lost and apprehensive.

'Look,' said Ramon, opening his wallet and taking out a piece of paper. 'My papa say, I see you, I give you thees.'

It was a small very faded newspaper clipping, I recognized, from an old pre-war Trinidadian newspaper, with a story about a canefield worker in Barrackpore who had been acquitted of a serious wounding charge, after chopping a fellow worker with a cutlass. Self-defence had been proven; there were many witnesses. I sighed. These things were never forgiven out in cane country, I knew. The courts might acquit you but people never did, no matter how much time had passed. Somebody had eventually made him out in the newspaper photograph. I finally knew why Lalchan had come to Port of Spain so suddenly years ago, and why he had departed equally abruptly a decade and a half later.

I took the young man in, of course; how could I not? He was a quick learner, like his father, and soon started a thriving small business, buying and selling household items. Then he opened a small retail establishment on the busy St James main road. He bought a small car and offered to take me to the beach on weekends, but I always refused, protesting that my knees were acting up and that I couldn't get into and out of his car comfortably. I let him take me back to our family home in Caroni once, though; it was still there, but had been sold by my sisters, leaving me out of consideration. I didn't mind; they had become virtual strangers anyway.

Now that I am retired, I take my walking stick and go for a stroll every now and then. King George the Fifth Park is a nice place to walk, but I have to be careful of the traffic in St James, which has become horrendous. It has also become very noisy; there are bars and rum shops at every corner, and people gather in the streets arguing about politics, women, steelband competitions, whatever they feel to argue about. I stop and listen sometimes, but I try to get back home in daylight; the people on the street are not those I used to know, and they don't recognize me or say good evening. There are lots of mixed couples and children on the street as well, I have noticed. Jasodra---- my aunt, my mother------ what would she have made of all this, I wonder.

Ramon cooks at home for me these days; his girlfriend, a nice Chinese girl, comes in and cooks as well. Sometimes they bring food that they have bought in some restaurant. I don't mind, as long as they don't bring beef or pork. I tell people Ramon is my nephew. Lalchan would be proud of how his son turned out, I think.

ROBBERY WITH VEE

The Boys

'Aye, where you find he?' asked Razor dismissively, chewing on his toothpick as he sat on his favourite perch, the wall under the streetlight at the corner of Penitence Lane and Coronation Street.

'Is a pumpkin vine family come up from Cedros,' said Teeths, introducing Valentine to the gang. 'He Tantie put him out. Say he getting outa hand, and she can't afford to mind him no more. I just pick him up by City Gate.'

'You and he is how related?' asked Reds.

'My mother is some kinda relative to he mother, I think,' said Teeths. 'Third or fourth cousin or something.'

'So where he mother?' Tallboy enquired. 'He don't have a mother?'

Valentine shrugged. 'She leave long time and went America.'

'And where you father?' Razor put in, 'you don't have a father or what?'

'I never meet he,' answered the new arrival. 'He leave my mother when she was pregnant.'

'So you is an orphan,' said Fellows, to no one in particular. 'No father. No mother. What you could do, boy?' he asked, turning to Valentine.

'Well,' said Valentine, 'I could cook little bit. I used to pitch

112

marble in the country and run race. I is a champion footballer too.'

There was an uproarious laugh from the entire gathering.

'He mean if you have any real talent,' said Teeths. 'You know, you ever put down a work where you come from? You ever do a small job or anything?'

'Well,' said Valentine hesitantly, 'the pickings wasn't very good. In my village, if you wanted to make an extra dollar or two, you had was to go outside, in Fyzabad or Princes Town or something. After a while you is a marked man. Everybody does pull out and go elsewhere. To besides, Tantie was real pressure. She say she woulda call police for me if she catch me in any slackness. It had some fellas I wanted to run with regular, but Tantie woulda bound sell me out.'

'Boy, like your Tantie don't understand how rough it is for youth these days,' said Razor.

'Yeah, boy, My mother don't even take me on,' said Teeths. 'All she on is prayer meeting and complaining how tired she feeling and how sickly she is. The amount of sick she say she sick, I swear I go reach home one day and find she fucking dead.'

'You ain't finding no regular work up here either,' said Tallboy. 'Wherever you go, they asking you for papers or if you skilled. If not, is dog work they giving you, with dog pay. And that is if you even lucky to get a work in the first place.'

'No respect,' added Fellows. 'No damn respect.'

'Boy,' said Reds pensively to Valentine, 'mighta be best if you did stay down they. Down country I hear people does help each other out with food and thing. But up here we does have to go and take what we want from them who have but not sharing.'

'That is what Teeths telling me,' said Valentine. 'But don't fool yourself. Country not like how it use to be longtime. Everybody for theyself these days, just like up here, it sounding.'

'These days you have to make it on your own,' said Razor. 'Is only one real friend you have…this.' He took out a revolver that was concealed under his shirt at the waist. 'This, and your pardners. Nothing else. Nobody else.'

'Sometimes I does wonder if it have another way,' said Reds philosophically. 'None of all you don't think it have a better way to live than how we going? If we not hiding from police, we fighting with other gangs. Some of we not going to make thirty years, all you realise that?'

'That is a funny way for you to be thinking these days,' said Razor. 'Some of the boys did tell me you getting fucking soft. You getting soft, Reds?'

'Nah,' Reds mumbled, 'but I does think about it these days. Is what them fellas does write in the papers say. Most of we go dead before thirty. I is twenty four. I wondering if I go make thirty.'

'And?' said Razor

'Nothing, nothing,' said Reds, detecting the quiet menace in Razor's tone. 'I good. I was just talking.'

Razor said nothing. Fellows and Tallboy looked at each other.

Valentine looked around. 'Well, I was wondering if all you fellas had a space for me. I ain't have much experience, but I willing to learn.'

'It don't happen just so,' said Razor. 'We have to check you out first. See how you perform under pressure. Then is initiation. But don't worry 'bout that now. Teeths, you and he is family, so you show him the ropes. Put him on a CEPEP gang to start with. In the meantime, the rest of we go check you out. You better be straight up with we.'

'CEPEP?' said Valentine in surprise. 'You putting me to cut fucking grass and thing by the road?'

'Is that same CEPEP here does keep we going sometimes,' said Tallboy

'Ain't CEPEP is only work every fortnight? I hear the money not so good,' said Valentine.

Razor smiled and lit a cigarette. 'The money good if you know how to work it,' he said. 'You go to work in the morning, lime for ten minutes than go home. Better still, get somebody to go for you, or sign for you. But the best thing for fellas like we to do is get a contract. If you could get a contract, your business fix. But it have plenty competition for contract. Sometimes it not safe to get a contract.'

'Yeah boy,' said Tallboy. 'Last week Pipers get shoot in town because he was fighting Duke for contract.'

'Pipers was dotish,' said Razor. 'You don't go looking for contract in other people territory. He shoulda stay where he did control things. Like how we moving up here.'

Valentine picked up the small, battered suitcase he had borrowed from a neighbour in Cedros.

'All right. Well, let me go and put this suitcase by Teeths. I coming back just now.'

Valentine and Teeths turned to head up Penitence Lane.

'What you say your name is again?' Tallboy enquired, as they walked away.

'Valentine.'

'Valentine. That is a girl name. Up here we go call you Vee instead.'

'That okay by me,' replied Valentine as he and Teeths began the sharp incline up Coronation Street, avoiding the large clumps of asphalt dumped then ignored like political promises on the road at irregular intervals, and the minefield of cracks and potholes that assaulted vehicles and the occasional pedestrian alike whenever they failed to exercise due care and attention.

Pastor Browne

'How often I telling you people, the day is at hand? It right here in the Bible. There will be weeping and gnashing of teeth, the Bible say. All the sinners and all the evil men will be cast into everlasting fire. They will suffer forever in Hell. But I tell you, brothers and sisters, it is still not too late. There is still time to turn your back on your sinful ways, and to follow the way of the Lord. He will forgive even the most unworthy. All he want is true repentance for your wicked deeds.

And you know that He will see if you are truly repentant. He have eyes to see into your very soul. He know all of you, all of you who have committed fornication, all of you who have robbed and killed, all of you who have sinned against His holy name. Beware the wrath of the Lord, the Bible say, beware the day of final judgment when He will come on a chariot of fire to seek out the just and punish the evildoers. Where will you be standing on that dreadful day? Will you be among those He will call and say "Stand on My Right" because you are saved? Or will you be among those cast into the burning pit to burn forever in torment?

You, yes, you my brother, where will you be? And you, sister, will you be in the Chosen Few? Do you think you will escape God's judgment? Read it in the Bible. "But you have a hard and stubborn heart, and so you are making your own punishment even greater on the day when God's anger and righteous judgments will be revealed." Paul to the Romans. Read it yourself. The Bible does not lie.

And if you continue to hide and protect the wrongdoers among us, then you too are guilty of the crimes they commit. If they have robbed, you have robbed. If they have fornicated, you too have fornicated. If they have killed or wounded, you too have killed or wounded. So I tell you, give them up. Chase their evil spirits from among us. Cast them out of your lives. The day is at hand. I am John the Baptist come again to tell you the day is at hand. Repent. Repent.'

Pastor Browne stopped and mopped his brow with his handkerchief. He noticed that one of the candles he had placed on the sidewalk had gone out. As he bent down to relight it, he took a surreptitious look at the collection plate. His audience had not been generous.

He had chosen his corner carefully, where the taxi drivers and maxis from the city, reluctant to proceed up Coronation Street, stopped at the Reliance Street junction and disgorged their passengers, leaving them to walk up the street by themselves unless some friend or family member resident in the area stopped or came to offer a lift. He saw them all as they passed, young and old. He too had lived up the hill once, until he felt the call and began spreading the messages he got from God every morning now as he bowed his head in intense prayer. Good fortune and the generosity of his itinerant audiences had made it possible for him to get a flat in one of the government-built Reliance Street 'plannings' a few blocks lower down.

But he had pitched camp at the corner of Coronation Street and Reliance Street, close enough to his former haunts to enable him to hail out many passers-by by name. It was also opposite Ma Jorsling's Tea Shop, not open in the evenings when he began his sidewalk services, but with an eave that offered shelter during the rainy season. He knew Ma Jorsling well; she had operated that tea shop ever since her husband died twenty years before, and he had become a regular morning customer, walking the few blocks from his apartment to have some bake and smoked herring with coffee, or to sit at the solitary small corner table with a fish pie or two on Friday mornings when the tea shop became especially busy.

Besides, he had his eye on Sandra, who had recently started to help Ma Jorsling early every morning, and whose ebony skin and tight-fitting clothes stirred primal impulses within him whenever he looked at her. Sooner or later, he thought, I would make myself known to her formally, and she would see the value of having a God-fearing man as a companion instead of those wayward young loiterers whom she seemed to fancy and with whom she chatted so easily.

Ma Jorsling

Ma Jorsling was up earlier than usual that Friday morning. Her neighbour's cock had begun crowing earlier than usual, fooled perhaps by the streetlamp which had suddenly flickered back to light after months of darkness. One day I going to wring that blasted fowl neck, she said to herself. Still, she wasn't too annoyed. Fridays were always busy days in the little tea shop she ran down at the bottom of Coronation Street; most of the fortnightly Council employees had been paid on Thursday evening, so a few would be coming to settle their outstanding debts. Because she served fish pies only on Fridays, she would have additional customers as well. Her fish pies were popular; in fact, she had once had a small write-up in the daily newspaper about her fish pies, and she had seen a bounce in her sales. But despite pleading from customers, she sold the pies only on Fridays.

She looked at her son Arnim sprawled on the sofa in her small living room, and the bedraggled heap of shoes and clothing on the ground nearby. She shook him by the shoulder.

'Arnim…Arnim. Wake up and help you mother little bit, nuh?'

Arnim rolled his head slightly, opened a bloodshot eye briefly, looked at her, then turned his head away once more and went back to sleep.

She thought of shaking him again but decided against it. He was an unwilling assistant in her business venture at the best of times, and on the rare occasion that he did choose to assist, his abrupt manner often turned customers away. He lived elsewhere with a girlfriend, but sometimes, if he had visited friends or gone out on a heavy binge and didn't want to drive home, he would crash on the sofa of her tiny bungalow on Purgatory Lane. His heavy snoring told her he wouldn't be happy if she insisted on trying to rouse him from sleep. Still, she noticed he had put money on the dressing table, as he always did. She was thankful for that; other women in the yard complained bitterly that their sons and husbands had spent all of their wages before they got home, and a few were occasionally beaten when they dared to complain too loudly or too persistently.

She put what ingredients she had already prepared carefully into empty cardboard boxes. Fish here, cheese there, potato over there. The hops bread she had bought the evening before were all in large paper bags. She had left the saltfish, onions and tomatoes down at the shop; she would make the buljol there as well and slice the salami and the large block of cheese for sandwiches. She was tired, having worked till just before midnight, but if Sandra came early to the shop, they might be able to fry some corned beef and smoked herring as well.

She looked out the window to see whether Joseph had come with the taxi. He plied the Carenage route, and always had to leave early, which suited her. For a small weekly fee he carried her and her assorted pieces down to the shop before he went to the Carenage taxi stand. She looked back at Arnim, still snoring on the sofa; if he was a different son, she thought, she wouldn't have to depend on Joseph early every morning to take her to the shop. Still, she reflected, he wasn't a bad boy, just a lazy one. Lord alone knows what he does spend his days doing, she sighed.

She heard the car pull up and the quick beep of the horn. She began picking up her bags and boxes and headed out into the gloom of the early morning.

The Benjamins

'Rodney, you not getting up this morning?'

Rodney Benjamin groaned as his wife drew the curtains open and let the early morning light flood the room. 'What time it is?' he mumbled, his eyes still closed.

'Half past six,' said Eileen, pulling the blanket off her husband. 'If you want to avoid traffic, you better get yourself in gear. Next thing you know, you reach on the site half hour late and all your workmen gone home.'

'Not today,' said Rodney, dragging himself to a sitting position on the edge of the bed. 'Today is payday. I could bet a million dollars every manjack turning up to work today. Early, to boot.'

'You want coffee?' asked his wife. 'Or you will wait until after you bathe? I making Spanish omelette this morning. I see the recipe on the internet last night. Hurry up in the bathroom, okay? Remember I have to bathe too, so don't use out the hot water.'

Having hot water was essential in the valley, Rodney thought, as he lathered himself in the shower. As a boy, he had never had the luxury of showering in hot water; he remembered his mother pouring a calabash full of ice-cold water from the barrel in the yard outside over his body, and he shivered instinctively. Poor woman, he thought; he had intended to take her away from the squalor of life in the barrack yard when he first started working years ago. But by the time he had moved up and become a small contractor able eventually to afford a small house in the valley, she had succumbed to the many illnesses life had inflicted on her.

'You take the cheque from my briefcase?' he asked Eileen when she came out of the bedroom dressed for work.

'Yes. What time you passing at the bank to collect the envelopes?'

'I don't know. Early, I think. Your bank does be real crowded on Fridays, I find.'

'Well, most fortnight people does get they salary on Thursday, so plenty of them does come in the bank to change they cheque or collect some money. And every month end is pensioners too. When you going to start paying workers with cheque, by the way? I tired tell you is safer than carrying money for them in envelope.'

'Yes, I know. But it hard to pay construction men with cheque. Plenty of them don't business with banks. A few is occasional workers, to boot. They don't want no cheque; they like the feel of cash in they hand.'

Rodney was grateful that his wife was a bank employee. He didn't have to line up and collect cash and sort it out in front of people. She did that for him securely, in a back office. All he had to do was pass and pick up the envelopes.

He saw she had laid out clothes neatly on the bed for him: striped shirt, dark trousers, socks. She had even put a tie; she wanted him to look well-dressed when he came to the bank, even if she knew he would take the tie off and shove it into his pocket the moment he left the bank.

They locked the front door and headed for the car.

'Wait a minute,' she said, walking over to the rose bushes she nurtured so carefully in the garden at the side of the house. 'Look,' she said, 'a small bud coming out. Just now we going to see a few more.'

Rodney grunted. 'Quick, woman, we late. Let we beat the traffic.' He had brushed his teeth after breakfast but the taste of her Spanish omelette still seemed to linger in his mouth.

Their sports-utility vehicle started without a hiccup, and he dropped her in front of her bank twenty minutes later.

'I will pass about 9.30,' he said. 'That okay?'

She nodded and got out.

Business Arrangements

'So, let we go through this again,' said Razor, looking around. 'Reds, I want you inside, pretending to fill out form or something. Keep you eye out for the man with the brown briefcase. I go come in just behind him, so you could be sure is him, then I going back out and crossing the road. Don't do nothing, just wait for he to start going back outside and follow him outside. Stick close behind him, you hear? You is a backup for Fellows.

'Suppose he get suspicious?' Teeths asked.

'Reds only following him up to the corner. Then he crossing the road. Fellows go take over then. Fellows, you snatching the briefcase after the man turn the corner. Head for the car. Teeths and Tallboy go have the car running a li'l way up the street. Fellows, you jump in the car.'

'Suppose somebody play hero and try to interfere?' asked Fellows.

'I go deal with them, 'said Razor. 'Remember I coming behind. Nobody know I involve, neither Reds across the street.'

'What about the bank security?' asked Teeths.

'The tip-off about the briefcase man come from the security by the door. He not going to give trouble. The other one go be up by the tellers, he not seeing anything by the door. Tallboy, you driving, right. When Fellows jump in the car, drive like crazy. Don't stop for nobody. Teeths, you in the car with Tallboy. You have your piece?'

'Yeah,' said Teeths, taking his weapon out and displaying it. 'Right here.'

'So all I doing is just lookout?' asked Vee. 'Outside the bank?'

'Yeah,' said Razor. 'You get a soft work this time. You ain't ready for the heavy lifting yet. But is important work. Is you to call and say if anything odd going on? Like police car, or something. I check my contact at the station already, so it shouldn't have no problem. He say one patrol car break down and the Inspector does send the other to take his wife to the grocery on Friday morning. So we should be okay.'

'Where we meeting after the job? When we going to share the money?' asked Reds.

'I tell all you don't worry with that. Tallboy and Teeths know where to go. I go tell all you when is safe to meet. Remember, tomorrow morning, nine o' clock, I want everybody in place.'

The meeting broke up. Vee and Teeths began walking up Coronation Street.

'Where all you going when you all you finish?' asked Vee.

Teeths looked at him. 'You hear what Razor say. Don't think about that,' he said. 'You just go home. In fact, better yet, stop by Ma Jorsling Tea Shop. Keep an eye out for any police or strangers coming in the area after we finish.'

'You expecting them to come looking for we so quick?'

'You could never tell.'

'This thing starting to look real dangerous, Teeths. All you ever pull a job like this before?'

'Vee, you real nervous, oui? Control yourself. You have to be real calm tomorrow morning. If you nervous, you could spoil everything.'

'Last time all we do is stick up a Chinee shop in Caroni,' said Vee.

'This time is almost a bank thing. And it close to home. Even if is not the bank, it close enough to spell trouble.'

'Razor planning this one long time,' said Teeths, 'no going back now. He had was to spend some good money setting it up too, bribing security and paying off he police contact and getting the weapons. That is how it is. Big risk, big reward. I think is nearly sixty thousand or more the man will have in the briefcase.'

'That is all? Sixty thousand?' exclaimed Vee.' All of this for what, ten thousand each?'

'We not getting ten thousand each,' said Teeths, 'I don't think is even shares going down. You not getting no ten thousand for sure, you only here three months now. Too besides, Razor does usually have to give something to the Don, like a ten percent. But I like how you thinking already. Big.'

'The Don? Who is that?' asked Vee. 'First time I hearing about he.'

'The Don is the man does really control the turf up here,' Teeths explained. 'Nothing does happen without he say-so. Everybody who make a score have to run something for the Don. Is he who does control the guns and them and have all the contacts. That is the man Razor does kinda report to. Me and you have to take anything that pass. If was less of us, was a bigger share. But the boys ain't make a good score for a while. Any money is more than no money.'

He leaned over to Vee. 'I think Razor set this one up without the Don, so all of we could get something more. But keep that under your hat, you hear me?'

'You think this job really worth all this risk, Teeths?' Vee asked. Teeths shrugged his shoulders.

They continued walking in silence up Coronation Street to the rum shop near the Penitence Lane Corner.

The Tea Shop

Ma Jorsling looked with satisfaction at her almost empty display cases. With the exception of a few loaves and some slices of salami on one dish and what remained of a block of cheese on another, they were all empty. Business had been particularly brisk; the Council workers had been standing at her door well before she opened at 6 a.m., and her fish pies had disappeared within the first two hours. Latecomers, disappointed, had made do with the other breakfast sandwiches on offer.

She saw Pastor Browne sitting at the small corner table chatting earnestly with a young man she thought she recognized vaguely. She came from behind the counter and walked over.

'Morning, Pastor. Everything good?'

'Oh yes,' said Pastor Browne, looking up. 'Your fish pies was excellent this morning as always. I glad I reach early to get. And the coffee help wash them down perfect. That girl does make a good coffee. Tell her I say so.'

Ma Jorsling smiled. 'I happy to hear that. You know a satisfied customer is the best advertising you could get. And what about you, young man? You like what you get? I not sure I ever see you in here before, but you look familiar.'

'This is Valentine Edwards,' said Pastor Browne. 'He ain't too long move into the area. He living up by you, I think.'

Vee looked up at Ma Jorsling. 'Yes, I staying with my aunt and cousin up Penitence Lane. You from Coronation Street, no?'

'Yes, but higher up, Purgatory Lane. How long you in the area now?'

'About three months,' said Vee. 'I really from Cedros.' He looked anxiously at the pastor. 'You have the time?'

'Is 8.25,'Pastor Browne replied. 'You have a appointment

somewhere?'

'Yes, yes, I have to be somewhere for 9 o'clock.'

'You have a job?' enquired Ma Jorsling.

'No, no... I meeting some fellas down the road.'

'Okay,' said Ma Jorsling. 'Let me take those for you,' she continued, picking up the plates and cups on the table. As she straightened up, she saw someone standing at the doorway, looking inside furtively. She recognized the face. 'Razor,' she said sharply, 'you want something?'

Vee swung around and looked at Razor standing there, his cap drawn low over his eyes. He was startled, but Razor gave no indication that he knew him.

'No, Ma Jorsling, I good. Nothing for me.' Razor nodded to the pastor and continued walking, turning the corner into Reliance Street.

'I know that boy from small,' said Ma Jorsling to Vee and the pastor. 'Never thought he woulda come out so. Every Sunday he in Sunday School with his mother. One morning bright so he beat he father with a pickaxe handle and damage the man for life. They send him reform school. He come out worse than he went in.'

'Why he attack he father?' asked Vee.

'They say the father used to beat the mother regular. The boy too. I not sure, people round there don't talk much, but that is the story I get. Anyway, he is a real bad egg now. You keeping company with he up there?'

'I have to go now,' said Vee hurriedly. He drank the rest of the bottled juice quickly as he stood up then hurried out the door.

'What it was you and he talking 'bout?' she asked the pastor.

'Oh, nothing much,' said the pastor. 'He was telling me about where he use to live, and his Tantie, things like that.'

'I sure hope he don't end up with that bunch up the hill,' said Ma Jorsling, shaking her head and walking back to the counter.

'I could get another coffee?' Pastor Browne enquired.

'Yes, sure,' she answered. 'I might close up early today. Everything nearly done. Coffee please, Sandra.'

The hot water kettle was whistling loudly when Arnim came through the door.

'What you doing up so early?' exclaimed Ma Jorsling in surprise. 'When I leave you was snoring like you wasn't going to wake up! You want something to eat?'

'Just a coffee,' Arnim mumbled. 'What time it is?'

'Just going on nine,' said Pastor Browne, as he came to the counter to collect his coffee. He put a teaspoon of sugar into the cup. 'You is Ma Jorsling son, right? You don't be in here often.'

'And how that come your business?' replied Arnim. 'Who you is, anyway?'

'I is Pastor Browne. I does hold little prayer meetings on the corner most evenings. You must come one evening.'

'Prayer meeting? What the ass wrong with this man?' said Arnim, turning to his mother.

'My son not too religious,' said Ma Jorsling quickly, handing Arnim a cup.

'That coffee smelling real good,' said a voice from the doorway

Rodney Benjamin came into the teashop and approached the counter.

'Mr Benjamin, long time no see. How you reach here this early morning? And you wearing tie to boot?' asked Ma Jorsling. 'Your wife cook another special for you again?' she added, laughing.

'Morning all. Yes, it have some kinda police block up the road,' Rodney answered. 'I waiting nearly half hour to come down the street. Some officer higher up tell me just take a park and wait till things clear up.' He put his briefcase up on the counter. 'I know I too late for fish pie. You better give me a cheese sandwich. This morning my wife give me something she call a Spanish omelette. I don't want to be unkind but I hope she don't make that for me again,' he said laughing.

'No problem,' said Ma Jorsling, placing cheese slices carefully into a loaf. 'Any pepper or mustard or anything? Sandra, bring a coffee for Mr Benjamin, please.'

Sandra steupsed. 'I was just getting ready to leave, Ma Jorsling. I thought you was going to close up.'

Ma Jorsling shook her head. 'All right, go ahead. I go make it myself,' she said resignedly.

She watched as her help took her small bag and left.

'That is the trouble,' she said to her audience of two as she delivered sandwich and coffee. 'She get pay this morning so she eager to go and spend she money. Whole week she telling me about some outfit she see downtown that she want to buy for some fete next week.'

'That is young people nowadays, 'said Rodney, taking the coffee and sandwich from Ma Jorsling. 'Spend it as soon as you get it. What you say, Pastor?' he said to Pastor Browne, whose eyes had been following Sandra as she flounced out of the tea shop.

'Yes, yes, of course,' he replied hastily. 'Some spending even before they get it. Spend, spend...nobody thinking about save, save...saving their soul for God.'

'Ease up, Pastor, is not time for service yet,' said Ma Jorsling. 'How the construction going, Mr Benjamin? You going to finish soon?'

'Is always hard to tell. I don't know when we go finish, maybe two weeks or so. I have to hand over by then,' said Rodney, lifting the cup of coffee to his lips. 'Is always the finishes does take plenty time.'

Arnim looked curiously at him. 'You is the contractor? For that office building down Reliance Street?'

'Yes, that is me, 'said Rodney with a trace of pride. 'Big job, but they choose me. I beat out plenty competition for that work.'

'I find all you real work fast,' said Ma Jorsling. 'Plenty of your workers does come here for breakfast every morning.'

Arnim swallowed the rest of his coffee quickly and headed for the door.

'Where you going so soon, son?' Ma Jorsling exclaimed. 'You just reach. What about some breakfast?'

'Don't worry, Ma Jorsling,' said Pastor Browne. 'Young people living on things other than food these days. He must be going after that young lady, your help. So, Mr Benjamin...that's your name, right? How business going these days? Long time I want to talk to you. It have some youngsters up here could use employment right now. Any way you could help?'

Friday night: The Benjamins

Eileen Benjamin took two slices of fish from the dish, placed one on her husband's plate and the other on her own.

'Fish in a special creole sauce,' she announced proudly. 'Was really lucky you didn't come the usual time this morning. I have a feeling is you them fellas was really looking to rob.'

'Could be,' Rodney replied, looking intently at the fish on his plate, 'but it look like the police know they was planning something. That is why they had roadblock set up and thing. By the time all the excitement finish, is only then I coulda get my car.'

Eileen chewed on her fish, then took a sip of water. 'Robert, the messenger, was in the road at the time. He say he had to lie down on the pavement when the bullet start to fly. Was like a small war outside, he say.'

Rodney sighed as he tinkered hesitantly with the fish on his plate. 'I wonder when all this robbery and shooting going to stop. Is plenty young people deading every day. Where they getting gun and thing from?'

'This country real going to the dogs,' answered his wife. 'People just trying to take everything you work for. All them young people dropping outa school, having baby before they could mind them, then have to kill and rob for money to live.'

'Some of them can't get jobs,' said Rodney. 'That self me and Pastor Browne was talking about this morning.'

'Pastor Browne? That quack? I hear he don't even have no religious training. Never even went to a Bible school or nothing. You like the fish?'

'Really?' Rodney replied. 'He sound really interested in getting jobs for young people up by Coronation Street this morning.'

'Where you see Pastor Browne this morning?' asked Eileen.

'Like I tell you earlier, when the police block the road and I had was to park up, I went in the little tea shop on the corner. He was there. We end up talking. Then the boy run in and we hear about the shooting.'

'Boy? What boy?'

Rodney rolled his eyes. 'I don't know he name. He was talking with Browne earlier that morning, Ma Jorsling tell me. He is the one who come back frighten and say they have a big shootout down Reliance Street. He was real shaking.'

'I could well imagine, 'said Mrs Benjamin, taking her last spoonful from her plate. 'My heart was beating fast fast when Robert was telling we what he see. I was real frighten myself. I didn't even go out for lunch. That boy you send for the envelopes, what he name, Brian? Is he had to go and get a roti for me to eat before I give him the wages to carry for you.'

'Yes, he tell me. Was late, but at least I pay the workers. Nobody grumble.'

Mrs Benjamin got up. 'I going to turn on the TV,' she said. 'The shootout bound to be on the news. You still ent tell me if you like the fish.'

Friday night: Ma Jorsling

Ma Jorsling walked slowly to her door. She had bought a few supplies for use on Monday on her way home from the hospital.

'Arnim? You home? Come and give me a hand!'

There was no answer. She put what she had inside, went back to the taxi, paid the driver and collected what remained. Indoors, the day's events had left her listless, without energy for work. She didn't know any of the boys except casually, dropping in for a quick sandwich or coffee. It was sad for young people in the community to continue dying before they even experienced life. And so violently.

Sandra had been lucky, hit by a stray bullet, but seriously enough to send her to hospital. And poor Razor. She didn't know what else to think now that he was dead. She had seen him just that morning by the tea house. Now he was gone. He and the other two.

She sat down for a minute, then heard muffled voices in the yard. She went to the door. Arnim was standing at the rear entrance to the barrack yard, speaking to someone.

'Arnim? You didn't hear me calling?'

Arnim looked at her over his shoulder, took the visitor by the shoulder and jerked his head. The visitor left.

'Who was that? I only catch a glimpse, but it look like one of them boys from up the road. Miss Cumberbatch son. What's he name again?'

'It wasn't nobody,' Arnim grunted. 'Mind your own business.' He went inside, clearly annoyed.

Ma Jorsling knew better than to aggravate him further. He was a strange boy, she thought. He didn't talk too much, at least not too her, and she had no idea how he earned his living. But she had learned to cope with his bad moods. After her husband had died, he had assumed responsibility for looking after her, even though he had moved out of the neighborhood to an apartment in the west. He had tried often to get her to move out, promising to put her in better accommodation. She had always refused. My navel string bury here, she said, and I don't think I could live in that fancy apartment you have. Besides, I have my tea shop. He told her often that she didn't need to work there anymore, that he would provide, but she refused. The tea shop was hers; it was what helped her to keep going after his father's death.

She began unpacking her parcels. Reds, she suddenly remembered, Reds. That is what they call Miss Cumberbatch son, because of his lighter skin and sugar-coloured hair. I wonder what business he had with Arnim, she thought, as she took the cheese and salami out of the second bag.

A telephone conversation

'Hello? Hello? Yes, is me. What's the news from up there? Any new developments? Yeah, that normal. Every time somebody get shoot on the hill they does light candle along the pavement. As though them fellas was some heroes. Yes, the girl all right, is just a shoulder wound she get. She leaving hospital by Monday. How you mean, why she get shoot? How the hell I know? Hear what you asking now, who shoot she. Was a shootout, everybody was shooting, she just happen to be in somebody line of fire.

What? No, we not looking for nobody else. Is Razor we had was to take down, everybody know that. I don't know why them others so stupid to look for fight. Yes, I know they thought was money. You really think we would send a plainclothes out there with real money. And no protection?

He gone back Cedros, you say? When? Last night? Well, he lucky he was outa the big action. He better stay in Cedros for a while.

Keep a low profile yourself, you hear me? But we curious to know who might try to take over that patch now. After Razor, who was next? The two in the car? Them dead. Who else? The snatcher? We have he in custody. He not going anywhere soon. Let we know if you hear about anything else, though.

I know, I know, you have to be careful. But send information the usual way once you hear anything.

Yes, yes, we pay the apartment rent for the whole year. Okay, good. Talk later.'

WATERLOO

The traffic rolled by in a ceaseless current, and for a moment, not seeing her as he came out of the Covent Garden Station, he thought she had decided not to meet him after all. Then he saw her, walking against the tide, dressed in her familiar yellow jumper.

'Hello,' she said, 'have you been waiting long?'

'Not really. I hadn't realized there wasn't a stairway at Covent Garden. There was quite a queue for the lift.'

He found himself hurrying to keep pace with her crisp, purposeful steps. She looked at him.

'Do all West Indians saunter along as you do?' she asked.

'I was about to ask if all Londoners walk as quickly as you do. But looking around, it seems they do.'

It had rained in London that morning. The grey blanket smothering the city offered little promise of sunshine. His fingers were cold.

'May I put my magazine in that rather large bag you're carrying around?' she asked.

He laughed. 'All my worldly possessions,' he said, then added, 'Just joking. It's my overnight stuff from the train last night. Plus my passport. Just in case. Let me have the magazine.'

They lunched at Tutton's, making light-hearted banter with the waitress who finally came to serve them after they'd been sitting for over a quarter of an hour. They spoke, about life in general, and what it was like working for the same accounting firm, but he was really watching her soft brown hair, so tantalizingly close to him, the hypnotic grey of her clear eyes and the tantalizing perfection of her London accent.

'It was a beautiful production,' he suddenly heard himself saying. 'I didn't much like The Winter's Tale at A Levels, but seeing it performed by a professional theatre company makes so much difference.'

'But I love The Winter's Tale!' she exclaimed. 'It's so…tragic!'

'That's your romantic streak,' he said. 'It ends happily, after all.'

'I'm decidedly not romantic,' she protested. 'I'm a cynic.'

'Inside every cynic lurks a disappointed idealist,' he said. 'Somebody said that. Can't remember who.' But even as he spoke, he noted how her eyes creased at the corners when she smiled, and the warm infectious way the twinkle in those eyes seemed to embrace him, and the way the melody in her voice seemed to reach his ears and his alone.

After they had roamed the stalls and shops of Covent Garden Market, haggled over the gifts each felt compelled to purchase, watched the buskers and mimics and three black girls playing steelpans in front of a banner that read 'Alternative Arts Theatre', they walked along Aldwych and down to the river. Leaning over Waterloo Bridge and looking into the soiled brown waters of the Thames, he suddenly remembered the River Queens of TS Eliot's The Waste Land, and just momentarily felt a sudden sadness.

As he had done every morning since his wife had died, Deonarine got up at 2am, washed himself quickly then said his prayers before the small tableau on his dressing table with images of Mother Lakshmi, Lord Krishna, a brass lota with hibiscus flowers picked the night before and a small photograph of Mahatma Gandhi off to one side.

Then he brushed his teeth, washed his hands, put a kettle on the kerosene stove and took a look around his small kitchen. He had soaked the channa the night before, adding just a little salt and turmeric as he had seen his wife do. Now he skimmed the scum that floated at the top of the pail with a ladle and threw it into the sink. He changed the water then put the channa on to boil, adding split lentils to the pot. He would add curry powder, more turmeric and other seasonings later.

He then took down the large cast iron pot from the wooden shelf above him, added oil and put this pot on the chulha he had constructed many years ago, when they had first decided to make and sell doubles for a living. He had put wooden kindling in the evening before, so he just had to put a lighted piece of newspaper in and watch the flame catch before adding a few coals. When the oil was hot, he would begin frying the balls of dough he had also prepared the night before and stored in the secondhand fridge he owned.

He had reduced the number of doubles he would make and sell daily to what he felt he could comfortably manage. When his wife was alive, she had been a bundle of energy, pushing him to help her do as much as he could ; the business had thrived, and mounted on his bicycle with the large lined box fitted securely into the specially constructed metal frame above the front wheel, he would venture far and wide beyond Waterloo village, stopping whenever someone hailed him out to serve up his family brand of the popular street snack.

He had heard that a number of other people were now setting up semi-permanent stalls, complete with large umbrellas and additional cooler filled with bottled soft drinks. He didn't feel inclined to burden himself and his bicycle with further weight; he had, on at least two occasions, pushed his bicycle back home from some distance away when a tyre had gone flat and had not relished the experience. His teenage son Kishore had come to meet him the second time, walking a mile or two up the dusty country road and helping as best as he could to keep the wounded bicycle moving forward.

Ten years later, Kishore was in London England, his wife had passed away, and Deonarine cycled out on his bike only so far as the shady almond tree that spread its broad leaves at the junction of the main road and the dirt trace that led to his home. The customers who knew him also knew where to find him, and sought him out every morning, from 7am to 9.30 am, by which time his stock had been sold out. He had been asked to come out again in the evening with his special brand of doubles, but he no longer felt the need to drive himself.

Money had long been safely put aside for Kishore's education, and now that he was alone at home, he found that his own needs had gradually diminished. Every two months he went to the bank in Chaguanas and filled out the transfer forms as guided by the bank teller to send pounds sterling to his son in London. He was barely able to read and write himself, but he was determined that his son would make his mark on the world. It was what the wife would have wanted, he thought, as he slapped channa onto a still-warm bara, lathered it with a sweet sauce and slight pepper, placed a second bara on top and handed it to his waiting customer

'That's where my father works,'she said, pointing to the South Bank. 'He's an actor with the National Theatre'

'Are you very close?' he asked.

'Not anymore. We used to be, closer than he was with my brothers. Now, I'm a disappointment to him—to both my parents. They think I'm immoral.'

'Because you have live-in relationships with men?'

'It's difficult for them. I'm twenty-seven. My mother thinks I ought to be married and having children.'

'Most children are disappointments to their parents,' he said.

'They all want to relive their lives vicariously through their children, but with enhancements along the way. It's the same in the West Indies, you know. But that is probably why you feel so desperately this need to be married.'

She hesitated. 'It's not just that. The Jewish woman is the backbone of the family. Without her, the family loses its centre. But that places such a burden on us, to live a life in which your decisions are inevitably influenced, if not made, by others.'

'It's the same with Indian families in Trinidad,' he said. 'But the responsibility falls on the shoulders of the first son. He becomes the one on whose shoulders all expectations fall.'

'Like you? Don't you have siblings?'

'I have two sisters. One got married and went to live in San Fernando. The other quarreled with my parents long years ago and went to live in Canada. She doesn't keep in touch. She didn't even turn up for my mother's funeral.'

On the river below, a police launch was moving slowly to shore. Two barges linked together crawled upstream. A tourist ferry crammed with sightseers emerged from under the bridge on their right. They waved at one who was pointing a camera in their direction.

'There's something I want to ask you,' he said suddenly, turning towards her. 'What chance does this have of going anywhere? I mean, what would you bet on an Indian from Trinidad and a Polish Jew from England beating the odds?'

'I think the bookmaker would win,' she said simply. A silence descended and they both looked at the imperturbable Thames swirling past beneath them.

Deonarine held his son's hand tightly as they walked along the main road in Waterloo. There wasn't much vehicular traffic, apart from the occasional taxi driver hired to make a special journey; the odd bullock or cow might break free of its tether and wander unrestrained in search of fresh forage. He stopped at an opening to a narrow causeway, little more than earth and rocks piled together, jutting out into the sea. Kishore covered his eyes from the glare and looked at the small white hut he could just make out glimmering in the afternoon sun at the end of the roughly constructed walkway. Tattered bits of coloured cloths attached to bamboo poles fluttered limply in the breeze.

That is Siewdass kootiah, he told his son, that man build this thing way out in the sea. With no help. He alone.

But why he build it out there, Kishore asked. Why he didn't build it on land?

Is a long story, his father replied. He did start to build it on land, but the Company take him to court and make him pay a fine and take jail because it was on their land. Their land! Was a piece of swampy land wasn't being used for nothing. That man make a jail for trying to give we a place to say we little prayers and thing. They come with a bulldozer and rip down the place. Mash it up! But God don't sleep.

What you mean, the boy asked.

The white man was driving the bulldozer, a tree fall on him and break he back. Siewdass did warn him was a holy place.

They walked along the causeway to the little white hut jutting out into the sea. Only now could he see that the building was still unfinished in places, and that the white distemper used to paint the walls had not been evenly applied and that there were discoloured patches here and there. Kishore looked at the water on each side, and the small waves breaking rhythmically against the small platform on which the temple had been constructed. It go get wash away, he told his father. The sea will mash it up. He looked anxiously at the brown water threatening not only to engulf the platform, but which beat incessantly at the coastline, north to south, ebbing and flowing with a monotonous regularity. He build it here because he say it remind him of the Ganges, said Deonarine.

Look, he said, look the man self coming. Kishore turned and saw a man in the distance coming towards them riding a bicycle. Two large buckets dangled from his handlebar. He nodded to father and son as he came up to them. Ram, Ram, he said in greeting.

Is rock and sand, old brick and cement that man does be carrying on that bike, said Deonarine, as they began walking back. He always improving the place whenever he could.

Nobody helping him, the boy asked.

I don't think he want any help, said his father. That is like his calling. Some special voice in his head reminding him where he come from, reminding him not to forget.

As they walked, Kishore looked back at Siewdass emptying the contents of his buckets onto the causeway, and at the brown waters swirling impatiently around. Then they were home, and he smelt his mother's cooking, and realized how hungry he had become.

'Look,' he said, pointing to the river. 'Isn't that a body they're towing in?' The police launch was shepherding something alongside that looked like a heap of old clothes.

'I don't think so. Surely they'd put it aboard, wouldn't they?'

'Must be a tyre then,' he said.' Certainly looks like a body'. He shifted his gaze to the dome of St Paul's Cathedral, clearly visible in the distance despite the weather. 'Have you managed to sort out what's going on between you and your boyfriend?'

'I don't know. You've caught me in a state of great personal confusion.'

'You want to get married but he doesn't, is that it?'

'I'm not sure that he doesn't, it's just that he's not sure himself. Perhaps he doesn't feel ready to cope with that responsibility. Personally, I think he's just immature.'

'Whereas you think you're becoming an old maid?'

'I need to give my life stability, direction. I don't want to be having children at thirty-five.'

'But he is Jewish, and respectable...?'

'Yes. He writes a political column for the newspaper. He owns his own flat. He is the son-in-law my parents would like to have. Would your family approve of me?'

'Hard to say. My father is an Indian man who has lived all his life in a rural village in Trinidad surrounded by people like him: sugarcane workers, farmers, fishermen, peasants. He sells doubles for a living from a modified old bicycle at a streetcorner.'

'Doubles? What's that?'

'A kind of street food. He sends me twenty pounds every two months,' Kishore laughed. 'He still thinks of me as a needy student. Like so many other Indian people, he thinks that white people are God's gift to the backward peoples of the world. Village Indians are circumspect around foreigners, but because you're white, they'd give you a pass.'

'That's so unfortunate,' she sighed. 'All this furor about race and class. I hate the very word discrimination.'

'But you're here because of Hitler and the Nazis decades ago. Discrimination exists all around us. When God, in His infinite wisdom, punished man's impudence by inflicting the curse of diverse tongues upon him, I'm not sure He realized how much further we would exploit that singular difference. In our great perversity, we have managed to create new barriers between ourselves: religion, race, geography, ideology. We fail to achieve what we can become as human beings. All our relationships are constantly battered apart by these obstacles of our own creation.'

'You're becoming too philosophical for me now', she said. 'What do you do with the money your father sends?'

'I save it in a special account. I would like to buy him a ticket to come to England. But first-class.'

'I'm sure he would enjoy it. Would I enjoy Trinidad?'

He thought for a moment. 'You'd like the informality, the sunshine, the beaches, the friendliness of people. You will see it as relaxing, quaint, different from England. But after a while you'd scream to escape. You'd miss the variety of London. Here you have theatre, pubs, the hum of life, your ability as a woman to live a free and independent existence. Most of all, perhaps, you'd miss the intellectual ferment that life in London offers.'

'Is that what has happened to you?' she asked. 'After, what is it, ten years of life in London, you feel you won't be able to re-adjust to life back home?'

'Yes,' he said sombrely. 'Now I inhabit two worlds but belong to neither'. He looked down at the river. What else floated up and down that mighty waterway daily, he wondered.

Deonarine felt tired. He was also sweating profusely, and he had felt his arm stiffen suddenly when he was lifting the box onto the bike. This thing getting heavier every day, he thought to himself. He had been under the almond tree since 6 am, and he was still not sold out. He looked at the cooler on the ground nearby. He had finally come to an arrangement with Miss Dalrymple, the nearby shopkeeper to take a few soft drinks and a bag of ice from her every morning, returning the unsold drinks to her and paying for what had been sold. This morning, like every morning these days, he had half-lifted, half - dragged a cooler full of ice and soft drinks to his spot under the almond tree.

He had been advised to add the soft drinks to his menu by customers who told him that similar vendors elsewhere were benefitting from bottled drinks alongside their doubles. Others were also diversifying into also selling aloo pies, dhal pies, even saheenas and kachoris. He knew he couldn't offer such variety, but the drinks were a useful add-on for which he was grateful, especially for the old-timers who had known him since he began selling, and who would stand around having their doubles on the spot, washing them down with a cold Solo or Coca Cola.

The conversation around his bicycle varied as it did from day to day from local gossip to world news. Sometimes local politics cropped up, and Deonarine listened half-heartedly as his customers alternately lambasted the government for its neglect and anti-Indian policies even as they criticized the opposition for its failure to make any significant headway outside of its traditional base. For Deonarine, politics was a remote and insignificant activity, with no impact whatsoever on his daily life except when the annual budget was read and he could learn about its impact on how he lived and survived. Even the closure of the Caroni Sugar Company the previous year had not affected him, having long retired from work in the canefields in favour of his independent existence as a doubles vendor.

'How your boy in London going?' asked Lall, one of his regulars.

'He good dey,' Deonarine answered. 'Last time he call, he was working in some big office by the river. Is some months ago he tell me that.'

'He don't call more often? He don't write you?'

'Well, is problem with the phone, boy, I don't have one so he does have to call the neighbour and I tell him I doesn't like to trouble them. So is only now and then.'

'He doesn't write neither? You sure he ain't have no white girlfriend now and done forget about you?'

Deonarine smiled and shrugged his shoulders. 'Who knows? But I don't read so good,' he said. 'It ain't have no family around to read any letter for me no more. The wife uses to. She coulda read.' He turned to a new customer. 'Slight or medium pepper?'

The boats and barges had disappeared in the distance. He looked over towards the police pier.

'It is a body,' he exclaimed. 'Look.'

A huge plastic sheet had been brought out and laid on the ground. For a moment, the spectre-white body, rigid, frozen in a grotesque clutching posture, hung in mid-air. Then it was lowered onto the plastic sheet.

'That's awful,' she said, turning away.

Later, sitting on the terrace benches, he looked back at where they had walked from the middle of the bridge to the South Bank. From here, he thought, the Thames seemed less murky, less intimidating. Far to the left, the Houses of Parliament, formal and stately, marked the start of a grand sweeping curve of imposing buildings that stretched along the banks of the great waterway.

'I must go now,' she said. 'I promised the girls I'd help them with the dips for the party tonight. You are coming, aren't you?'

'It might be a bit uncomfortable for all involved, don't you think? He'll be there, won't he?'

'Yes, but I'd be terribly disappointed if you didn't.'

'We'll see. I do need to go back to the office for a while. Are you parked nearby?'

'Yes, come on. I'll give you a lift. There's very beautiful old Jewish synagogue in London,' she said. 'Would you like to see it some time?'

'Are non-believers allowed in?'

'Only those from the Caribbean,' she answered.

They pulled up at Liverpool Street Station and he opened the door. The noise of trains filled the air. He turned to her. For a brief moment, as he leaned over and kissed her, he felt in the moist warmth of her lips all the promise of a life begun anew. He turned and walked into the station, and saw the ordered carriages, linked and silent, and further on, the intricate criss-cross of the network lines, and heard the announcements over the public-address system. He thought of looking back but felt himself sucked into the vortex of human traffic hustling impatiently to and from their trains and he knew for certain that the moment had gone.

When he got to his office, his assistant had left a telegram on his desk. He looked at it and saw it had come from Trinidad.

There was no one around his cart when the flashy rental car pulled up alongside and a young well-dressed Indian man wearing expensive designer shades came out.

'Morning, Uncle. You're Deonarine, right?'

Deonarine nodded. The young man had an unfamiliar accent.

'I glad to find you,' said the young man. 'My Dad always talks about you and the doubles he used to buy from you. I came looking for you once or twice before, but people say they wasn't seeing you any more in the area.'

'I doesn't travel out from round here anymore,' said Deonarine apologetically.

'Dad said your bara was the softest and your channa the tastiest he ever ate. So I know I had to try your doubles out whenever I come to Trinidad.'

'You don't live here?'

'Nah,' said the young man, 'I'm from Winnipeg. Born and grow up there. My Dad, he's still there, but he don't feel to travel long distances anymore, so he don't come. He sent me to fix up a few

business matters for him. He had some land here in Waterloo. Somebody's buying it from him, so I've come to fix up everything. Lemme try one of your doubles, then. Slight pepper.'

He watched as Deonarine placed the channa on the first bara, covered it with condiments then placed the second bara atop the mixture. 'We have doubles in Canada too,' he said. 'But I hear it's nothing like the real thing. That is what my Dad says. He don't eat Canadian doubles, you know. He had one once; dumped the whole thing. That was the first time he mentioned Deonarine doubles from Waterloo. Nearly fifteen years I waiting to taste your doubles.'

'What your father name?' asked Deonarine, watching as the young man tried to manoeuvre his way around the delicacy.

'Hassan,' said the young man, using a paper napkin to wipe the curry that was sliding down his fingers. 'Shit!' he suddenly exclaimed, as some curried channa spilled onto his shirt. He wiped at the spot furiously, then stopped. 'Uncle, my Dad was right. This is a master doubles! Hit me again.'

Deonarine dutifully obeyed and watched him as he dispatched the second doubles in a matter of seconds. 'Hassan?' he said. 'That name sounding familiar. He use to live around here?'

'Yes, a long time ago,' said the young man, helping himself to a soft drink. 'Farouk Hassan. He changed the name when he went Canada. Now he is Freddy Hassan. Was easier for the Canadians. I'm Freddy Hassan Junior. Everybody calls me Junior. Listen,' he continued, 'my father says to see if the temple by the sea still standing. I have to take pictures for him too. It's near here?'

'Not far,' said Deonarine. 'Drive down the road little bit. Is on your right. But it kinda break down now. Since the old man dead, nobody really looking after it. Is Hassan you say your father name? Farouk Hassan?'

'Yeah,' said Junior. 'I'm heading to the temple now. Mind if I took a picture of you here too? My mother and father asked me to take your

picture if I saw you.'

Deonarine nodded and stood still, holding on to his bicycle as Junior took his photograph.

'By the way, where's Suchit Trace?' asked Freddy Junior, moving the camera from his face.

'Right here,' said Deonarine, gesturing to the trace that led to his home. He turned to point. He felt strangely light-headed, and his fingers suddenly began to stiffen.

The phone rang just as he was leaving the office. 'You haven't come yet,' she said. 'Aren't you coming any more?'

'I won't be able to make it,' he said, holding the phone close to his ear because of the music and chatter he was hearing in the background. 'I have to go back to Trinidad in the morning.'

'When?' she said. 'Has something happened?'

'I leave tomorrow,' he said. 'My father has fallen ill suddenly.'

There was a silence. 'I'm so sorry to hear that,' she finally said. 'Is he in a hospital?'

Kishore hesitated. 'Yes, I'm sure he is. I really don't know. They didn't say.'

'How terrible. Are you all right?' Do you want me to come over? What dreadful news.'

'No, it's okay. I have to pack. Besides, you have your party tonight. I'll be fine.'

There was further silence. 'Eli has proposed,' she finally said.

'Did you accept?'

'Not yet. I told him to give me some time. Do you know when you'll be back?' she asked.

'No. Not really. I've called my boss. She said I could take as much time as I needed. I must go now. Much to do.'

'Please be safe. Oh, how sad...'

'Take care,' he said, before he hung up.

The middle-aged lady at the edge of the small gathering looked vaguely familiar so he walked over to her. 'You look familiar,' he said to her. 'Have we met before?'

She looked at him. 'Kishore,' she said softly. 'Boy, you get so big.'

He recognized her now. He remembered climbing on her lap asking her to read to him.

'Sushilla,' he said quietly.

'Yes,' she said. 'That is your nephew over there. The one in the black shirt with the fancy shades.'

Kishore looked over and picked out the youth.

'He name Freddy,' she said. 'Is in front of he he collapse. Just as he was taking he picture. Look.'

She reached into a small purse she was carrying and took out a Polaroid photo. Kishore looked at his father standing under an almond tree next to his bike with the doubles box securely in the metal frame.

'He and the shop lady put him in the car and take him to hospital but was too late.'

Kishore nodded. 'I could keep this?' he asked, pointing to the photograph.

'Well,' she stammered, 'is the only picture I would really have of him. Is a long time, you know, and I leave sudden.' He understood and handed the photograph back to her.

'What happen there?' asked Kishore. 'Nobody ever tell me. What happen between you and Ma and Pa? All these years you never visit. Why?'

She hesitated for a minute. 'Is because I was pregnant,' she finally said. 'I did want to get marry but they was real against it because he was Muslim. Me and Farouk went Canada right after that and get marry. I send letter and thing but they did always come back. Look,' she said, showing him an envelope addressed to Deonarine Singh, Suchit Trace,Waterloo. 'All come back. "Address unknown". Come and meet Freddy.'

After the cremation they dropped him off at his father's house. It was as he remembered it, a simple wooden structure, partially on stilts. His father had enclosed a section downstairs to use as a bedroom, probably unwilling to climb stairs as he grew older. He passed his hand on the small counter with pictures of Mother Lakshmi, Lord Krishna and Mahatma Gandhi.

After a while, he walked down the road to the causeway leading to Siewdass's kootiah. The site had fallen into serious disrepair. The causeway itself was crumbling away, the stones, sand and broken bricks collapsing under the pressure of the elements. The little mandir itself had lost part of its roof, and patches of the walls once so carefully constructed of mud and thatch had fallen off in clumps. The sea still swirled and lapped greedily at the platform and along the brown sand.

He thought of the man on the bicycle laden with buckets of sand and gravel, and of another man on a bicycle selling doubles under an almond tree, and of rivers that lead to the sea, and of the oceans that keep people apart. He stood there till the sun went down in the west then walked back to the house in Suchit Trace.

(author's note : in 1995, the Siewdass Saddhu Shiv Mandir in Waterloo, Trinidad, known as the Temple in the Sea, was reconstructed after years of neglect and re-opened as a place of worship. It draws numerous visitors to the site every year. A statue of

Siewdass stands at the entrance).

PASTELLES FOR CHRISTMAS

Two Saturdays before Christmas, the ladies of the Mendes household converge as usual on the family home in Woodbrook to begin the ritual pastelle making for Christmas. This started as an annual event some ten years earlier, when youngest daughter Marisa, newly married, overheard her husband telling a friend on the phone how much he was looking forward to having a Mendes pastelle with his garlic pork for breakfast on Christmas day.

'What to do, Mom?' she asked her mother, close to tears. 'I never tell him is you does make all the family pastelle every Christmas. Now he go find out and we only just married. It too early for quarrel in the marriage.'

Daphne thought for a moment. 'This can't continue,' she said. 'I wouldn't be here forever. Besides, this pastelle making is a very time-consuming work these days. Call your sisters- in -law, Lana and Savi. Is time all of you start making pastelle and everything else for yourselves.'

Making pastelles is really time-consuming, Marisa has realised. She hadn't been part of the ritual when she was a teenager and young adult; her life had initially been focused on the parties she could attend on Friday nights, boozing on expensive drinks at Club 52 or elsewhere, or mashing up the place at Panorama and fetes by Machel,Kes and the big all-inclusives. This rich vein of activity left her incapable of waking up in time to help her mother make pastelles.

Then for two years, she and Adrian had become part of a regular expatriate Saturday morning bram on Maracas beach. Yes, she thought, her mother really had it hard those many years frying the minced pork and beef, pressing the dough, wrapping and binding them in the singed banana leaves then boiling them all by herself until the others began chipping in to help. Ten years later, married with two children, she has become not just the inspiration for but a devoted core member of the Mendes Pastelle -making Foundation.

'What we going to do,' Daphne announces when all the ladies are gathered,' is the usual assembly line like always. I go make the dough and form the balls. Savi, you could flatten them in the press like every year. By the way, where my son your husband? He not coming this year'

Savi is apologetic. 'Matthew real heavy into this new religion he pick up. He say he can't mess with pork. Pork unclean. So I not taking any home this year. But I come to help.'

'Pork unclean?' says Elena. 'He eating pork all his life and now he find out it unclean?'

'Well, I find so meself, but he is the man of the house, so I have to let him go the way he feel to go,' Savi replies reluctantly.

'And that,' says Elena, a triumphant note in her voice, 'is why I never marry. Them men too boldface, want to have things their way all the time,'

'I thought was because no man wanted you,' says Lana. Lana is the elder of the daughters-in-law, and enjoys a fairly senior position in the clan, having married Raymond, Daphne's older son and eldest child, an airline pilot, who now seems to be constantly called up by the airline to fill in for some absentee pilot or another.

'I wouldn't go there,' says Elena. 'Stories could come out that you wouldn't like.'

'Enough, enough of this idle talk,' Daphne interrupts hastily. 'Bring out the pastelle press, Elena. And you, Marisa, go in the fridge and take out the olives, capers and raisins, and put them in bowls on the table. In that order, olives first.' She goes to the stove and brings over a small pot of cooked meat. 'I already season and cook the pork and beef and mix them together. Savi, where the fig leaf?'

'Oh shit,' says Savi, 'I forget them in the car. Wait, let me go and get them.'

'You singe them already? 'Daphne enquires.

'Yes, yes, last night.' She hurries out the door.

'Country people always damn forgetful,' says Marisa. 'Once I invite she and Matthew to go to the beach with me and Adrian. You know what time she reach? Nearly two o'clock. She forget to tell Matthew, she say, and she had was to wait for him until he come home from doing market and grocery.'

'Wait, he does do the grocery and market?' asks Elena. 'Ma, like you make a real mamapoule man dey.'

'He ain't no mamapoule man,' says Daphne. 'Matthew was always a helpful boy. Very kind, thoughtful, considerate. Shhh...,' she whispers, as Savi re-enters, the bundle of banana leaves half-obscuring her face.

The table is laid out systematically. Cornmeal dough at one end, shaped into small balls, followed by the pastelle press with a bowl of oil and plastic wrap at hand. Meat next, then all the extra ingredients laid out in sequence. Finally, the singed leaves, the string, the aluminium foil. Daphne looks it over. Yes, all is well and in order.

'Raymond say he want an extra dozen this year, Mom,' says Lana.

'He give one or two to his boss last year Christmas and the boss ask if he getting any from him this year,'

Elena snorts but says nothing.

'Well, you know what Raymond want, Raymond will get,' says Marisa. 'That is the first child, the first boy. Special treatment always, not so Mom?'

'I don't know what you talking' bout,' Daphne replies tersely. 'I treat all my children equal. No preference for anybody.'

Lana, Elena and Marisa snort collectively. Savi busies herself wiping down the pastelle press and putting a splash of oil on its flat surfaces. Elena wraps a bandana around her head.

'Okay, let we start,' she says, after she has tied the apron string behind her. 'What we waiting for?'

The process begins smoothly, and after a while develops a regular rhythm. Press, fill, sprinkle, wrap, press, fill, wrinkle wrap. Silence drapes itself uneasily over the proceedings.

'Savi, how your sister Jasodra going? You ain't tell us anything about she for a long time', Marisa remarks, spooning a few chopped olives, raisins and a caper or two onto the meat covered dough before her. Savi hesitates.

'Why you want to know people business so?' asks Lana, noticing that Savi hasn't answered immediately. 'Is farse you farse so all the time?'

'I not farse,'replies Marisa sharply. 'If anybody farse, is you, always minding people business. Anyway, Savi is family, so I was just trying to keep up with family matters. You know, with the children and thing, I wasn't really keeping up with everybody.'

'Adrian was the only thing you was keeping up or what?' Elena comments, to laughter all around.

'Jasodra okay,' says Savi finally. 'You know she married now?'

'She marry? I thought she did just run away from home with the man,' says Daphne.

'And it was a black fella, no?' Elena interjects. 'I know your parents didn't like that at all.'

'No,' answers Savi quietly, 'they didn't like it. They didn't like that she pick up with a coloured fella, they didn't like that she run away with him, they worse of all didn't like that she ups and marry him.'

'They musta feel real shame,' Lana volunteers. 'I know Indian people, especially them from the country, don't like black people at all. And worst of all, a daughter? Lord have mercy.'

'They didn't even go to the wedding, although she invite them,' says Savi sadly. 'They send and tell she to come for she clothes. When she reach, they didn't even let she come inside. They put all she clothes in some black garbage bag and pelt them over the bannister for she. Matthew had to go and help she pick them up from the road and put them in the car and carry them home.'

'That real sad,' says Daphne, 'real sad. Thank God that don't happen with Potogee family.'

'Really?' Elena is quick to retort. 'You wasn't so happy when Matthew marry Savi. Why you bringing country bookie Indian in the house, you tell him. Remember?'

Daphne reddens. 'That was before I get to know she,' she chirps quickly, putting an arm around Savi's shoulder, and ignoring the slight wince she feels. 'Now she is the best daughter-in-law I could have.'

'Well, I glad to hear that,' notes Lana. 'Next time you have to go to the doctor, is best you call she and not me or me husband.'

'Your husband never even in the country,' cackles Marisa. 'Besides, you know what she mean. She not comparing all you. She just saying she really like Savi now. Look out! You just wrap the same pastelle twice!'

'My husband is a pilot,' Lana responds testily. 'At least he working day and night to feed he family. He not living free in he mother house.'

"Yes, he working day and night,' Elena interjects. 'Especially night.'

'What you mean by that?' Lana says. 'What it is you really trying to say?'

'Who, me? All I say is that Raymond putting in plenty overtime. Plenty overtime. He really putting it in overtime.'

'Anyway,' Savi continues, as though speaking just to herself, 'anyway, Jasodra having a baby just now. I wonder what Ma and Pa going to say.' She sighs.

'Baby is a wonderful thing,' says Daphne. 'Watch and see. Once that baby born and the grandmother see it, all is forgiven. Mark my words.'

'Will be a dougla child,' Lana murmurs. 'I not too sure about that. It have some Indian people living down the road by me...'

'All you excuse me for a minute,' says Savi suddenly, 'I have to go to the bathroom,' and she stops pressing the balls of dough and walks off quickly.

Daphne rebukes them. 'You see what all you mouth does cause? All you upset the girl.'

'All you? Who start this old talk in the first place?' says Marisa. 'And don't try to blame me. All I do was ask she how she sister doing.'

'Is time for a quick break anyway,' Daphne replies. 'How much pastelle we do so far? Thirty? We still have at least another thirty to go.'

They all step back from the table.

'Anybody want a drink?' asks Elena, as she washes her hands at the kitchen sink. 'Mom have a nice bottle of port she get for she birthday. Straight from Portugal. Raymond bring it for she after he make a flight there this year.'

'Well, I like you,' exclaims Daphne in mock annoyance, 'offering my birthday gift to other people. Alright, Elena, go and get it.'

'Mom,' says Marisa quietly to her, as Elena leaves the kitchen, 'you think that is a good idea? You know how Elena does be when she have a few drinks.'

'Is just one drink,' Daphne answers. 'Is Christmas time. This is the only time all my girl children does really get together ... without they husband. One little drink wouldn't hurt. What you think?' she asks Savi, who has returned to the kitchen

'Is your daughter. You know best. But you know is only one drink it take to trip she off,' Lana interjects.

Elena returns with the bottle of port. She has already opened the bottle and checked its contents for smell and taste. Now she ceremoniously begins pouring a drink for everyone.

Savi declines. 'Not for me, please, I don't drink alcohol, you forget?'

'A most interesting family,' Elena announces, emptying her glass in a single swallow. 'Husband not eating pork again, wife not drinking. If all you was Catholic, sainthood could be on the cards.'

'Plenty people don't drink,' says Lana, sensing an opportunity. 'As a matter of fact, it would be better if some people didn't drink so much, or more people didn't drink at all.'

'I'm afraid I just don't get your drift,' snaps Elena, affecting the tone of an English aristocrat she had seen in Downton Abbey the night before. 'Is there some message you trying to send us, my dear?'

'When I have message to send, I does deliver them direct,' Lana replies, 'I don't put water in my mouth to say anything.'

'All you ready to start back?' Daphne enquires quickly. 'We still have nearly three dozen to do again.'

'You does deliver them direct to your husband, my darling brother Raymond? Or you does send them to one of he outside woman?' Elena, a second drink warming her up, is preparing for combat.

'If my husband go outside looking for woman, that is he business. He is man. I don't know about other people going outside looking for woman, especially when they is woman theyself,' Lana retorts.

'What you trying to say?' challenges Elena. 'What you trying to say? Come out and say it.'

'It have nothing for she to say,' said Daphne hurriedly. 'What wrong with all you today?'

'If I did know it woulda be this kinda lacouray, I woulda stay home,' Marisa complains. 'I didn't come here for all this. Elena, why you does have to bring up stupid talk every time we get together?'

'Stupid talk? What stupid talk? Everybody in town know Raymond horning she night and day. Is only she don't want to admit it.' The third drink has now fired Elena up to fever pitch.

'If I wasn't in your mother house, me and you woulda have a ringdong here today,' Lana exclaims.

'Ring dong? Ring dong? If is fight you want, I ready right now,' says Elena, raising her voice.

'All you stop this nonsense now! Stop it, I say!' Daphne is becoming visibly upset.

But Lana has become too upset herself to hold back. 'Don't take me for one of them woman friends you have who you think you could beat up when they leave you for somebody else,' she declares, but in a tone that has suddenly become menacing. 'Stick to your drinking and cool off.'

'Easy, Lana, easy, 'says Marisa, 'things really getting too hot in this kitchen. You, Elena, go inside and cool off. Lana, go outside a bit and smoke one of your cigarettes.'

'I stop smoking,' Lana mumbles. She has cooled down immediately now that Elena has gone inside.

'That's what you want us to believe,' snickers Marisa. 'We know you start back. Go ahead, take your cigarette break, but outside. You know Mom don't like smoking, especially in the house.'

'Yes, your father used to smoke like a chimney. Is that what give him the lung cancer that kill him. Kill him and leave me to mind four children.' There is a trace of bitterness in Daphne's tone. 'No wonder I had trouble with all you. Raymond a playboy, you a party girl, Elena...well, Elena didn't like how your father treat me and his children. Anyway, the man dead, so let we not badtalk the dead.'

'Elena shouldn't drink at all,' says Savi quietly. 'You know she have a drinking problem.'

'Don't say that! Don't say that at all! My daughter don't have no alcohol problem. She have a few personal issues, that is all, and she does have to have a little drink every now and again to ease she mind. Nothing wrong with that. I does have one meself when I ready.'

'Yes, but...' Savi stops when she sees Marisa looking at her with her finger to her lips.

'When we going to finish these pastelles now?' moans Daphne, composing herself quickly.

'Don't worry, Mom, we could always finish them another day if we have to,' Marisa reassures her.

'No, no, they have to finish today! No sense putting all these things back in the fridge. Besides, the leaves will dry up and get useless. No, today. You all could leave if all you want. I go finish by myself. I accustom.'

'Finish what by yourself?' asks Lana, who has just come back in and has only heard Daphne's last sentence.

'You smoke that real fast,' says Marisa. 'Mom was saying she would do the rest herself, but I don't think so. I will stay and help her.'

'Me too,' says Savi. 'This is something we always doing together for the last few years and we shouldn't mash that up now. This might be the last time we could do this, who knows?'

'I staying too,' says Lana. 'More hands make light work.'

They arrange themselves around the table once again.

'I will do the wrapping and tying, 'says Daphne, 'since Elena not here. Savi, you will have to make the balls from the dough, then press them out. Actually, let we make all the balls first now, before we start again. That way will be simpler.'

They all begin rolling balls of dough in their hands and laying them out in a rectangular Pyrex dish that Daphne has brought from the cupboard.

'Good, good,' Daphne says, 'we moving like clockwork now.' Savi is about to flatten the first ball into shape but she stops and gulps for air as if she cannot breathe properly.

'I have something to tell all you,' she suddenly says. 'Matthew and I getting a divorce.'

There is a deathly hush around the table. All work ceases. After a few moments, Lana becomes the first to speak.

'This is, well, terrible news you giving us, Savi. What happen?

You never tell us anything was wrong with the marriage. I thought you and Matthew was going good.'

'I don't believe this,' Daphne blurts out. 'My son woulda tell me something. Tell me you joking.'

'She not joking, Mom,' says Marisa quietly, 'you can't see the girl crying? Sit down, Savi. Tell us what going on. Perhaps we could help.'

They all sit down in a semi-circle. Lana holds Savi's hand and gives her a tissue. Marisa goes for a glass of water and hands it to her sister-in-law. Daphne sits in numbed silence.

'So tell us what happening, 'coaxes Marisa. 'None of us know anything about this. You have us in shock.'

'I going to call Matthew now,' Daphne suddenly says.

'Not now, Mom!' Marisa exclaims sharply. 'Come on, Savi, tell us what going on.'

'Matthew find a girl…a woman, in this church he going to now. He say he serious about her and want a divorce so he could marry her.'

'He say that?' asks Lana incredulously. 'He ask you for a divorce? Boldface so?'

Savi sobs but manages to tell them that Matthew came to her a fortnight ago telling her that he was now really in love with this woman, that they had a lot in common, and that he was going to move in with her and marry her if Savi gave him a divorce.

"And you agree?' exclaims Lana. 'Just so?'

'Well, I think about it a bit first, but I realise it have nothing I could do if that is what he want. He say I could have the house, the car, everything. That is when I realise that it don't make sense fighting it. He giving up everything for she. What I could do against that?'

'Who dead?' asks Elena, coming out of the house. She has had a brief nap and has washed her face as well. 'Why everybody looking glum so?'

Marisa explains.

'What shit you telling me?' Elena exclaims. 'Matthew? Matthew?' She turns to her mother. 'The loving considerate son?' She turns to them all. 'You see what I does be telling all you about men? Don't trust them. They is all despicable cheating bastards. They does take what they want then abandon you. Not so, Mom? Like father, like sons, eh?'

There is no answer from Daphne.

'What you going to do now?' says Lana sympathetically to Savi. 'You want us to talk to Matthew? You want us to try to knock some sense into his skull?'

Savi shakes her head. 'Is okay. Let things work out however they workout. I have some clothes pack in a bag in the car. When I leave here, I going by Ma and Pa. I don't know how they going to take this. First Jasodra, then baby, now this. It go kill them with shame.'

'You sure you don't want to come and stay by me for a few days?' asks Lana.

Savi shakes her head and refuses. 'I will be okay,' she says. 'If all you don't mind, I would like to leave now. I don't think I able to continue making pastelle right now.'

There is a long silence after she leaves. They all listen and hear the car drive off down the street.

'I hope she going to be okay,' says Marisa 'She was really upset.'

There is another long silence.

'Same thing I tell Matthew,' Daphne finally says. 'First sign of marriage trouble, Indian girl does run home to their parents' house.'

'Mom,' says Elena, looking directly at her, 'why you don't shut the fuck up sometimes?'

When she gets home, Lana is surprised to see Raymond there. 'How was the pastelle session?' he asks. 'Here,' she replies, 'your mother send the extra dozen you ask for. I putting them in the fridge.' He goes into the bedroom. When he comes out, she sees that he is wearing his pilot's uniform. 'Another relief shift?' she asks. He nods. 'I'll be back day after tomorrow, I think.' She watches him as he goes out the door, into his car and drives off. She closes the door and decides to call her friend Janice to decide what they are doing tomorrow.

Marisa pulls into the driveway of their home at Westmoorings-by-the-Sea and hears the children splashing about in the pool. She walks around the house, is greeted by loud cheers and is splashed with water. Her daughter's blond curls have stuck like plaster to her forehead. She moves them aside to give her a kiss on the forehead. She suddenly notices how the light makes her husband's body appear even more pale in the pool. 'Pastelles, anyone?' she enquires.

Savi pulls up in front of her parents' home in St Helena Village. It is one of those concrete structures standing on six pillars; the living space is upstairs, while below a solitary hammock made from jute matting swings listlessly. She takes a deep breath, lifts her suitcase and walks across the narrow wooden pathway that traverses the drain and leads to the house

Elena and Daphne are washing the dishes and tidying up the kitchen. 'Mom, you have to stop saying things that just jump to your mouth,' Elena admonishes her mother. 'Sometimes is better just to keep quiet.' Daphne doesn't reply. She dries her hands, leaves the kitchen and walks into the living room. She pauses before the framed photograph of her late husband on the mantelpiece where it stands next to the plaque that reads 'Bless Our Home'. Is alright, Vincent, she will never hear it from me, she thinks, as though speaking to him. She mightn't be your daughter but at least you keep quiet all the years, even though you never stop punishing me. Is alright. It go remain our little secret.

Elena walks past, looks curiously at her mother for a minute, puts on some parang music then disappears towards the front porch with her glass of ponche-de-crème.

END OF THE LINE

Sometimes when I hear a vehicle growling on the gravel on the driveway coming up, I does feel a little jump in my heart and I does say well, this look like it, my number finally call. Most of the time though is the garbage truck. This morning the garbage collector even hail me out. Aye, you still here, he shout, like you lost?

I like sitting out here in the porch in the early morning. I could look out, from this little bungalow high in these hills above St Augustine, to the plains below. Everything does seem so peaceful down there. This morning it had a drifting cloud that fall asleep during the night and forget to move on. Vaguely the distance it have this clump of blue, which I know is the hills of the Central Range. I don't see them as clearly as I use to; they tell me I have glaucoma, and that sooner or later I will go blind.

Blind? Another punishment for my sins? I does look across towards Mt St Benedict and think of all the stories of miracles I hear that happen there. But I know it have no cure for what eating me inside for so long, making me depress and tired all the time. God does never turn His back on you, the television preacher does continually repeat, reach out to Him and all will be forgiven. Lord knows how much times I reach out to that television set, waiting for that miracle to explode off the screen and give me an ease. But I think God forget about me a long time ago, and I ain't make it easier for him to find me over the years.

I does think back sometimes and wonder what happen when and why. I sure I wasn't born the way I is now. I don't remember being different from other children. I play in the road, pitch marbles, hide and seek like everybody else. Even when that Venezuelan boy Rafael take me under the guest house he was living in and put his hand on my penis, then make me put my hand on his, I remember thinking then that this was strange but fascinating. But that happen once, it never happen again (I think the boy went back to the mainland with his parents) and I continue as normal.

I really never like the rough sports, though. Football and cricket and wrestling wasn't for me. I used to enjoy painting and drawing more. I used to enjoy the fashion shows on television more too, and the dancing and singing. To me watching the beautiful creativity I see there make me want to copy them, so I start designing stuff in my school copybook and my drawing book too. I like writing stories too; my teachers used to like the stories I write when they give composition.

The more I think about it, is probably in secondary school that I start to feel I was really different from most of the other boys. But in big school you have to be careful. School is a real cruel place for people like we. The boys does find you out quickly and soon everybody does start calling you names and harassing you. I try to be as lowkey as possible. It had other fellas from the way they talk and walk, was a obvious giveaway, and is pressure they use to get. I keep to myself most of the time, but sooner or later water does find its level and I was soon part of that small group that discuss things that interested us quietly in a corner or some small room somewhere.

People have no understanding about gay people. They think we does deliberately behave in particular ways or does try to jump in bed with any man in sight. Is not so at all. Most of us want to live a normal, quiet life like everybody else. It have a few cosquelle ones, but it have cosquelle people who not gay too. But in them days if people only sniff you was a homosexual, was like you was the devil on earth, out to corrupt people children with your evil ways. In Church and religion classes, they pound into your head that homosexual people was curse and insulting to God. In the papers people use to write saying was a sickness and that people like us needed medical and psychiatric attention. God forbid if you come from some of them depressed areas; if they find you out, they beat you and put you on the street for people to mock you. No wonder we had was to lie quiet and go underground to meet and enjoy each other's company.

A man come by we the other day. I did never see him before but all of a sudden he reach and asking my father if he could stay a while by we. My mother and father didn't look too happy but they tell him come inside. I look at him real close up then. He wasn't really a man, just a young boy, maybe was eighteen years, but I was young, ten years, so he did look real big to me. Me and my brother Owad we stay in a corner while he talk with Ma and Pa; they did always tell we stay outa big people business so we stay quiet. But I get to find out, listening to the talk, was my father brother, and that he was hiding out from some people was looking for him. Out here in the country it real deserted; nobody does even come here, and it don't even have a road does come out here, just a dirt track, so if was hide he was looking to hide, he choose a good place. This is your uncle Hemant, my mother finally tell us, is your father brother. He come to stay with us for a while. But you is not to tell anybody, you hear? Don't even tell your friends in school, otherwise your father go beat all you bad. And don't say nothing to no neighbour or nothing. What neighbour, Ma? I ask, it ent have nobody else living round here. Don't mind that, she say, just don't tell nobody, all you hear?

When I finally decide to tell my parents that I was homosexual, I thought my father would kill me. He start ranting aloud, and slap me hard, his face red with rage.

'You telling me you is a fucking bullerman, eh? You mad or what? I didn't raise no son to be no bullerman, you hear me? Get your ass out this house, you hear? Get out!' And he begin shoving me, screaming. 'This is what I send you to school for? To lime and pick up faggot friends? Eh? Well let them faggot friends mind you now! Go, get outa here, before I kill you!'

My mother stand by silently, tears streaming down she face as I try to shield myself from the blows. Is the last image I have of the scene before I find myself in the street, the door slamming behind me. I was trembling. I put my hand to my face; my cheek was swelling already, and my lip was bleeding.

A few curtains in nearby houses was drawn, and curious eyes was peeping through the curtains to see what going on. I stand up awhile, not knowing what to do, then walk to the park and sit on a vacant bench. A vagrant, slouching on the bench opposite, raise his head, look at me, suck his teeth and turn away. I sit down gathering my thoughts, then call Jason from a phone booth. When he hear what happen, he tell me to come over right away so we could see what could be done.

'Shit, Kerry boy, your face is a mess,' he say when he meet me by the door. I take a quick look in the hallway mirror, see the burst lip and the swollen cheek, and turn away quickly.

'Here,' he say, 'put this ice on it.' I take the ice cubes he had wrap in a handkerchief and press them against my cheek.

'You could stay here tonight,' he say, 'but I don't think my parents will let me have a house guest any longer than that. They beginning to suspect something too,' he add, holding my hand in his momentarily. 'What you going to do?'

'I not sure,' I answer. 'I have some relatives in the country, but I feel my father done call them already and tell them not to take me in.'

'You mean he tell them that you... I mean, that you not straight?'

'No, I think he probably tell them some other story. He would be too shame to tell people that he have a gay son.'

Last night we hear some strange noise outside we hut. Like somebody was moving in the bushes nearby. Owad was still sleeping but I get up. My mother and father was awake, and my father put he finger to his lips and motion me to keep quiet. I didn't say nothing. I see my uncle, he name Hemant, looking out through a window. The house was dark; we didn't keep no lamp on in the night because my father say we wasting pitchoil. But it had moonlight and in the little light through the holes in the galvanise roof I see my uncle had something in he hand. I look closer and see was a gun. I get frighten one time. I never see no gun before in real life, just in pictures, but I recognize was gun right away. After a while, the noise stop. Must be was a wild animal, my father whisper. My uncle didn't say nothing, he just shake he head little bit and continue peeping through the window. I think he stay there till morning, because he was still there when I get up again in the morning to brush my teeth and eat my breakfast. You think we should send the child to school today? my mother anxiously ask my father. Yes, is best she go, my father say, try to act normal. So I put on the school blouse I had, take my book bag and start to walk. I know if I was lucky I mighta meet Boodram father taking him to school in he jitney so I woulda get a ride at least part of the way.

Jason send me by a friend who had a mas' camp there in Carlos Street. His name was Randolph, but everybody call him Boots. He was a real good designer; the costumes he make was always real original. I was with Boots for two years. Was my first relationship, and it wasn't bad. He treat me good and I had a place to stay in the camp. I use to help out in the night near Carnival making costume and headpiece and stuff like that. After a while I get a job in a bank, not far from Carlos Street, and start earning some proper money. It wasn't anything big, I was just a teller for the first six months, but they does move you around a lot in the bank so you learn about different aspects of the bank business, and after two years, I was junior supervisor.

Boots come and tell me one day that he going New York, so he have to close down the camp. Somebody up there offer him a good work designing for some fashion shows and small theatre productions, and he was really interested in taking up the offer. He was getting free lodging too.

'Anybody I know?' I ask him and he kinda smile but he didn't answer. I wasn't surprise. We wasn't as close as we used to be since a few months before, and I suspect he was seeing somebody else. I couldn't complain. I was seeing somebody too, a fella I meet in the bank. He had a small apartment right there in Woodbrook, and he was always inviting me to leave the mas' camp and come and stay with him. So it was a good opportunity for me and Boots to call it off.

'You must come and visit me in New York when I settle down,' he say the evening before he leave. I nod and shake my head but I know that was that. I wouldna mind going New York, for I hear it was easier for fellas like us up there, we didn't have to hide and pretend, it had bars we coulda visit and you could hold your friend hand in public and kiss if you want. But not in this country, not in this Trinidad. Police still use to raid one or two of the bars we used to hang out in, just for fun, and threaten to lock we up.

'In jail you go get plenty of what you like,' one of the corporals used to say. 'Black and sweet.'

But they never ever lock anybody up. That was because we had a big judge used to be in the place with us. Whenever he was there and the police come in, they used to be real apologetic. 'Our mistake, your Honour,' they used to say. 'We get a wrong tip-off.' Then they would start to snigger as they walk out.

When I reach home that evening only my mother and Owad was home. He was lying in the hammock sucking a bottle. My mother was taking up a few clothes she had drying on some stones outside.

She ask me to knead some flour to make roti, so I went inside and take off my school blouse, put on a home jersey, and start to knead the flour. Ma come inside a little later and begin to clean some bhagi she had pick from outside. Was nearly dark when my Pa and uncle come back. We arrange something with a fella in Carli Bay, he tell my mother. He go take him mainland tomorrow night; is only one day again. Ma look happy to hear that. She was looking real stress since my uncle reach. We eat, then I start to do my homework. Pa and Uncle Hemant went outside. My mother take the dirty wares and start to scrub them out with some dirt.

I didn't recognize was gunshot I was hearing. Was like somebody letting off fireworks. Then plenty shouting from outside. My mother start to scream. I hear a man bawl out 'Oh God!' My father come rushing inside. Run, he shout, hide. Then like somebody shoot him in he back and he pitch forward and he fall on the ground. I run in the bedroom and grab my little brother and run to a corner. I hear my mother screaming for mercy, then more gunshots. Two shadows appear in the doorway. One man look like he was pointing a gun but the other one say that is children, leave them, we get Hemant. I start to shake and tremble. The first man hesitate, then went away with the second man. Owad was crying now, like all the noise frighten him. I hear like the men walk around outside, then like they leave, but I was too frighten to get up. Is only after fifteen minutes or so I get up, holding Owad. When I do so, I suddenly realise I had pee on the floor.

When I went out I see my Ma lying flat on the dirt floor. Blood was coming from the back of she head and mixing with the red earth on the floor. It had a big hole in my father back, was blood all over the floor by the door too. I begin to feel sick. I didn't know how to cross over him to go outside, but I finally manage. Uncle Hemant was lying down in the yard outside. He had plenty holes all over his body, even his face. I was feeling to throw up, but I hold on to Owad and begin to walk like a zombie down the dirt track. I see some headlights coming and I stand up. I couldn't move. I thought they was coming back to kill me and Owad. Then I hear Boodram father voice saying 'Oh God, what happen here, chile? What happen here?

When you handling money like in a bank, temptation always in your face. I didn't think I was thiefing anything big. Sometimes when customers was making big deposits or withdrawals, it used to have a cent or two excess. All I use to do was round off the deposit and put the extra cents in my account. It was never big, and I never thought was something they was going to investigate. But one morning the manager come to me and take me to the meeting room and make me sit down. Then some auditor fella come in and start to ask me questions. I really couldn't get away, they did already pull up my account where I was depositing these extra cents and ask me to explain how I get these thousands of dollars. They ask me if anybody else was involve and I say no.

The bank wasn't biting nice. I get charge for fraud and theft. They give me two years. Why you do something like that, my mother ask. How I coulda tell she that the lifestyle I was living with nice apartment and clothes and night life, I couldn't pay for on my junior supervisor salary. I didn't have no defence so I get the full shaft. They even confiscate the money I was putting aside in that special account.

I was real worried about jail. They say it not easy for gay people in there; sometimes you even go in straight, you come out bend. When I was in the Remand Yard, three fellas corner me in the bathroom.

'Doo doo,' one say, 'you looking nice. You does behave nice too?'

'I know he,' say another, looking at me close up. 'He use to be with Boots. All you remember Boots? The buller in the mas' camp?'

'So he done break in already?' say the first man. 'He going to like it.'

'Aye,' a strange voice say quietly, 'the Boss say leave that fella alone.' I look behind the three fellas and see a short gnashy looking fella wearing a merino standing with a towel and a bar of soap in his hands.

'Wha' happen, like the Boss want him for heself?' said one of the trio grumpily. But they left and walk away.

'You is the banker fella,' said the newcomer. 'I name Chadee. The Boss have some interest in you. It have tings you could help him with. When you get out, you go meet him. Don't worry about them other fellas,' he say, jerking his head in the direction of the three who just leave. 'The Boss have you back now. You safe.'

I only realise how safe I was when another fella try to grab me a few days later. Two others suddenly come up and beat him bad. I was confuse but thankful. I prefer to choose my own partners.

They let me out one day to go to my father funeral. Two police went with me and I was handcuff. I stand up next to my mother. 'What happen?' I ask.

'Heart attack,' she say simply. 'Like your grandfather. All you have it in the genes.'

'My grandfather? My father never say much about him. He from Venezuela, no?'

'No, he wasn't from Venezuela,' my mother answer, 'he was from here, Trinidad.' She show me a faded picture of a man holding a toddler in his arms. 'This is your grandfather and your father. Is the only picture you father had of them together. They take it in Venezuela somewhere.'

'My grandfather was from Trinidad?'

'Yes,' my mother reply, 'his name was Lalchan.'

'How he end up in Venezuela?' I ask.

'He had to run from Trinidad,' she say. 'Your father didn't talk much about it. Some trouble with some girl, or some wounding, or both. He used to run with Boysie Singh too. Anyway, he marry a Creole girl and they run away to Venezuela. He dead, many years now, heart attack, like your father. Your grandmother pass away in Venezuela too, about ten, fifteen years. She live long.'

I didn't know nothing about my family history. My father always remain silent about it. I always thought my grandmother was the Indian lady he used to call Auntie when he take me as a child to see her in St James.

'So who Auntie was, then?' I ask. 'The lady from St James.'

'That was your grandfather good friend. When Ramon come to Trinidad after his father dead, he went to look for she. She take him in. He live with her for a long time, until we get marry.'

'So how come I have a Spanish surname, like Valdez? It shouldn't be some Indian name?'

'Your grandfather didn't have no other name, I think, just Lalchan. He add on the Valdez after a while in Venezuela. Was the first name he coulda think of, I suppose. It make things easier.'

I stop to take it all in. 'Well, look at my crosses,' I finally say. 'My grandfather is an Indian. My grandmother is a Creole. My father is a dougla. You...' I look at my mother, '...is a Chinee.'

'Half,' she correct me. 'My mother was Chinese. My father was a Yankee sailor who make her pregnant then went back to his wife in America. You know that already.'

'This Trinidad,' I tell she, 'this Trinidad. Is a real mess-up place.'

I think this was the first time I really start thinking that nobody could get away from what coming your way, no matter how you try.

I went back with the police. I serve my two years for bank fraud. They take off plenty time because of how long it take for my trial to come up. When I come out, Chadee was waiting for me outside the jail. 'Come,' he say, 'I have a place for you to stay. The Boss want to meet you too.'

I sit with Owad when the police come, three or four car, with blue and red lights. Some of them went in the house. A police lady wrap two blanket around me and Owad and tell we to sit in the squad car. She was kind. Boodram mother and some other neighbours come by the car and put they hand around me and say how sad they was. I hear them talking among themselves saying what a terrible thing this was, and how this was a nice quiet place until this and how my Ma and Pa was such quiet people who never trouble anybody.

I didn't say nothing, not even when the police with the notebook come and ask me if I could tell them anything about who it was and if I see they face and if I notice anything special about any of them. I just shake my head. I look over where my father was lying down in the doorway and how they was measuring something and walking around him. A man looking like a doctor come from inside shaking his head. I see my uncle Hemant on the ground with all the bullet holes and I wonder why he did have to come here and why he bring this trouble for we. I wonder why my Ma and Pa had to dead, since all they used to do was plant garden and sell in the market whenever it had a little extra.

Miss Boodram come and try to take Owad away from me but I hold him tighter and wouldn't let go. She was crying, I don't know why, wasn't her mother and father dead, but she had big tears in she eyes. Finally a man come and sit down next to me in the car. Was Ajodha the pundit. He didn't say nothing at first, he just sit down there. Then he start to talk to me about how bad things does happen and how sometimes you have to be strong and not to worry my Ma and Pa in a better place. I really wasn't listening too much. I was watching them take my mother out from we little hut in a black bag and put she in a white pickup next to my father. Then they pick up my uncle, the man who cause all this, and I know that if I was bigger and braver, I woulda get outa the car and run and kick and cuff him up even though he was dead already. But I didn't do nothing, I just sit there watching everything like if I was just a camera.

Me and Owad spend that night by Boodram house. Deo who was in school with me look at me all the time, but we never speak. Owad suck he thumb and fall asleep. I lie down but never close my eyes, I look up at the roof whole night, except whenever I hear Miss Boodram coming in the room to check on we, I close my eyes tight. In the morning Miss Boodram give we some roti and tomato choka; I pretend to eat but I didn't have no appetite. We going home now, Owad ask. Miss Boodram start to cry; Mr Boodram just stand up looking sad. Deo didn't go to school that day either.

My teacher and the headmistress come by the house later and try to talk to me, but I didn't answer them. I hear Miss Pierre say to Miss Jacob that I was in shock or something; I don't know what they was talking about. It had a lot of talk going on whole day about what going to happen to we and where we going to stay, especially as nobody know if we had any family. My Pa had a brother, I wanted to tell them, but he dead now. The police come back too, trying to find out information, but I had nothing to tell them so I remain silent.

The Boss didn't want me because I was gay, it turn out. He wanted me because I knew about banking and could help out not only with hiding his cash but with laundering it and helping him keep his accounts up to date. He sit behind his desk, looking at me from behind some dark glasses, as I explain how he could set up accounts under different names (you didn't need all the extra ID and utility bill and shit you need these days back then), how to organise cash businesses like groceries, gas stations and car parts places as fronts for washing your money, and how to manufacture fake foreign invoices so that he could send money overseas. He use to smile every time he hear something that he like, and I used to see the gold tooth in his mouth that earn him the name Goldfinger, like in the James Bond pictures. He really like gold; he had a big gold chain round his neck, and thick bracelets on his right wrist like Indian women does wear when they going out. I show him how to set up different sets of books for the different businesses he use as fronts for his drug business.

'Right,' he say, 'you working for me. But I telling you this once, and only once. Don't try to cross me. Don't ever t'ief from me. And if I ever give you a order, carry it out without question. You understand?'

I understand right away. I understand that if I didn't stay and work for him I was a dead man. That was my destiny. So I shake my head to say yes, and watch him smile. He give me a room in his mansion to stay, and a office to work in. That was special treatment; he didn't let his other men live in the house, not even his closest assistants. But I know was because he wanted to keep a close eye on me all the time.

I was working for him about six or seven years when one day a young boy come to the mansion with Teddy and Chadee.He had a clean, beautiful face, and jet-black hair. I fall in love one time. In all them years with the Boss, I didn't have a single affair with anybody. I was ripe for a romance.

'Who is that fella?' I ask Chadee when I get a chance.

'He name Hem,' Chadee say. 'Don't let his looks fool you. He is a deadly killer.'

'Killer? But he so young.'

'He only looking young,'Chadee say, 'he have twenty years. The Boss recruit him from somewhere down south. They say he done kill three people. But,' Chadee say, 'I hear he just like you. He is a homo too. I feel the Boss must be bring him just for you. Is alright,' he continue, looking at my worried face, 'the Boss don't have no problem with these things. However a man want to swing, that is he business, he does always say. Just as long as he do whatever he have to do.'

Hem and me slip quickly into a relationship, without the Boss saying anything. Hem couldn't stay in the mansion, he had to stay in the quarters the Boss build for his men some distance away, but very often he would come over and spend the night. I was hoping the two of us coulda pull up and leave, but deep inside I know it didn't have no chance of that happening.

One day I had to go to Port of Spain to fix up some of the Boss paperwork with a bank there. I was waiting for my appointment time on the chairs downstairs when somebody come and sit down next to me. He was dress very shabby and smelling funny. I pull away a little.

'Kerry,' he say, 'you don't recognize me? Is me, Boots.'

I look at him. I had to look real hard, because this man was thin for days, and had a scraggly beard.

'Boots?' I say. 'I thought you was in New York! What happen? You not looking so well.'

'I come back a few months now,' he say. 'Yes, I not feeling too good.' He leaned over. 'In fact, I come home to die.'

'What shit you telling me?' I say. 'How you mean you going to dead?'

'I have AIDS,' he say, tears in his eyes. 'I get it in New York.'

'But,' I say, 'they have drugs and thing they using to treat that these days.'

'I wait too long,' he say. 'Typical Trini. We feel God on we side and nothing bad could happen to we. Well, God laughing at me now. How you going?'

'I okay,' I say.

He look at me curious. 'Look,' he say, 'if you have time we could go somewhere and have some coffee or something.'

'I have a meeting upstairs,' I say. 'When it finish, I will come down and we could go.'

My meeting went on for longer than I expect. When I was coming down the stairs, I look up and see his reflection in the glass as he was walking out the doors. I didn't bother to follow him. How you go know what to talk about with a dead man walking?

My mother visit me last night. She come when I was lying down on my bed and stand up looking at me. Ma, I say, you come back. You not dead. She just stand up there looking at me with sad eyes. They take Owad from me, I say. They take him and put him in a home somewhere with strangers. How I going to look after him now? But my mother didn't say nothing, she just put she hand on my head then pull she ohrni tighter round she head, because it was fluttering madly in the breeze. Hold on, Ma, I going to close the window, I said, and I get up and went to the window, but when I turn around she was gone. Ma, Ma, I cry out, Ma, Ma. Then somebody hold me by my shoulder and start to shake me. Wake up, chile, you dreaming, wake up. The Sister was looking worried, because I was crying plenty now, first time since they kill my parents.

I does sit down in this garden for long hours. They put me in this place because Miss Boodram finally tell them that she can't keep we any longer because it really don't have no space and was getting difficult to mind two extra people, one being just a toddler. When they first try to take Owad from me, I hold him tighter. But one morning I get up and he wasn't around. They take him in the night. Sister say they take him to a nice family who would look after him proper. I didn't care. I scream whole day, calling my brother name. But that night was when my mother come and put she hand on my head and I get calm. After that I does just sit here in the garden counting the flowers and watching my mother and father laughing and talking together as they picking tomato and pimento to sell in the market.

A man they say is a doctor come to see me the other day. He try to talk to me but I know he want me to tell him 'bout my Ma and Pa and what they does tell me. But I not telling him anything. Last time they make my Ma disappear. Not again. So I does just sing them little hymn they teach we in school and some of the Hindi prayers my mother used to sing. Prayers does keep away bad spirit, she used to tell me. Sometimes when she come we does sing hymns and bhajans together.

'Somebody taking money from you,' I tell the Boss. 'The figures not looking normal. Some days they real low. You want to see?'

The Boss didn't say nothing. He just clench he jaw and walk away, but he come back half hour later. Show me, he say, so I show him. He didn't say nothing, he just pick up the books and went inside. Two days later, he come back.

'I think I find out who it is,' he say. 'I want you to go with the boys and bring him back. It have some questions I want to ask him.'

'Who it is?' I ask.

'The boys will take you,' he say. 'Tonight.'

I jump in the van about seven o' clock and we start to drive. Another van was following we. We drive about two hours, way out in the bush, over all kinda dirt road and patch-up pitch road. Was real dark when we stop.

'Here,' say Chadee, 'we have to walk from here. Down this track.'

I just barely make out it was Hem before they start shooting him and shouting. Another man sitting on a bench get up and try to run inside. Somebody with a shotgun shoot him as he run inside shouting and his back burst wide open. They was still shooting Hem on the floor although he look dead already. I stand up in shock for a second by Hem body then I hear a woman inside screaming. I jump over the man body in the doorway and run inside. I was too late. Dougla shoot she in she head just as I run inside. Chadee was going to the little room on the side. I went with him. It had two little children in a corner. Chadee raise he gun. 'Oh God,' I cry out, 'them is children! Leave them!' Chadee look at me for a moment then lower his weapon.

'Lewwe get outa here!' somebody shout. Everybody start to climb back in the vehicles. I stand up by Hem body, unable to move. Chadee come and drag me in the van.

We drive back in silence. I was feeling real sick. They had to stop to let me vomit then speed off again. I look at my feet. My pants and my shoes was cover with blood. Some get on my shirt, I don't know how. I keep seeing Hem body on the ground, riddle with bullet. And the man in the doorway. The lady in the house. And the terrify little girl watching me and Chadee with big eyes, holding the other child.

When we get back my knees was still shaking. Somebody had to help me walk. The Boss come to the door with a question in his face. Chadee nod and he went back inside. I went in the bathroom and try to wash the blood from off my hands and feet. I look at my face in the mirror and I had turn a pale color. I catch a glimpse of the Boss watching me from the doorway. When we four eyes meet, he walk away.

I try hard to concentrate on work the next few days but was impossible. I keep seeing Hem body, and them two other people, and every night I does get up scrubbing my shirt and sweating. I went and tell the Boss that I want a few days off. He watch me from behind them shades he was always wearing.

'Yes,' he say. 'No problem. You could go. Take how much time you want.'

'You is a real ass,' Chadee whisper to me when he see me with a little carry-on bag the next morning. 'The Boss don't like weak people. He feel you go sell him out just now. He not letting that happen.'

So is nearly a month now I in this little sanctuary up here in the hills. Is like a place where you could hide from the world. Some nuns does run it to help people with mental problems but who not dangerous, like a kind of therapy. But it have no therapy for the sickness I feeling inside. And every now and then, when I hear a car coming up the driveway, like I say, my heart does beat a little faster. But I not going to run or hide. Sometimes I wish I could be like this little girl it have here. She does sit on the porch with me sometimes, but she don't talk. Sometimes I does hear her singing and talking to some imaginary person in the garden. Poor child. If I did know them songs she singing, I woulda sing along with she too.

MR MAC : AN EPILOGUE

Every Sunday morning at about 9.00 am, Mr MacDonald Thomas would pass in front of our house on St Vincent Street on his way to church, accompanied by his wife. Unlike his working day apparel, usually light grey striped shirt and khaki trousers, Mr Mac would be dressed in a suit, a grey pinstripe or light brown affair, complete with waistcoat and tie. He usually carried a bible under his arm, and, in the rainy season, a large umbrella. His wife would be equally well-dressed, a benign smile on her face as her husband acknowledged the greetings of people on the street.

Mr Mac had perhaps the most cheerful disposition of any shopkeeper in our neighbourhood. Where Mr Teixeira was polite but remote, or Mr Biscoito always business oriented, Mr Mac engaged in endless banter with his customers as he sold them their goods, on cash or 'trust'; delinquent customers, those who had not paid their bills yet still wanted more credit, were reminded of their obligations, yet were usually given their requirements with seemingly gruff condescension which was recognised for the show it was. I suspect Mr Mac put on this stern face for the benefit of his wife, who sat on a stool nearby and critically monitored business activity, including the credit accounts.

Mr Mac's shop was a rectangle he had enclosed at the front of the building which also served as his house. A narrow doorway provided entry and exit between the shop and the living quarters. Along the side of the building was a driveway, leading to a storage area at the back where heavy and bulky non-perishables were stored, and where kerosene supplies were kept.

Two heavy-duty double doors, secured after closing by long iron bars that fitted into slots anchored in the wall, afforded customers entry to the shop. Inside, large crocus bags filled with sugar and white flour sacks of equal dimension lay one atop the other in one corner. This was also a choice spot for some customers or idlers who had no hesitation in sprawling across them.

A long wooden counter, four feet wide, ran the length of the rectangle, its surface smoothed by years of countless use. A red, old-fashioned scale, with a moveable brass tray and iron weights of differing poundage, rested on one end of the counter; anything from rice to butter had its weight determined on that scale. At the other end, a glass tray housed bread, heavily salted Norwegian brand butter drawn from a large tin, cheddar cheese and occasionally salami for the hungry who needed instant nourishment.

Activity in Mr Mac's shop was an endless buzz of dealing with multiple customers simultaneously, including going outside to fetch a multiple-gallon tin of cooking oil or to pour kerosene from the large drum into a waiting housewife's container. Stored in ceiling-high shelving at the rear of the shop were the hundreds of miscellaneous items that were part of the shop's inventory: zippers, matches, buttons, candies, paper bags, cans of milk powder, tinned meats, cheeses and vegetables.

You could buy ping-pong balls for table-tennis as easily as you could flannel-covered balls for lawn tennis or windball cricket. Open bags of dried lentils, red beans and black-eyed peas popped up here and there; coloured paper for making kites lay flat on a shelf, an open box with smoked herring was shoved under the counter, and salted codfish lay on a butcher's block alongside the small hatchet used to subdivide the larger pieces for individual purchase.

On Saturday mornings, my father went to Mr Mac's shop religiously with his list, prepared in his meticulously neat handwriting. The list seldom varied: ten pounds rice, ten pounds flour, ten pounds sugar, one bottle of cooking oil. One of us would accompany him to help bring the purchases back home. Later, when we were older, we would carry out the errand ourselves. After I had done this for some time, I arrived at Mr Mac's shop one Saturday to meet a sizeable crowd.

'Come, you big enough to do this for yourself,' said Mr Mac, raising part of the countertop and inviting me in. Thereafter, I did it routinely, always coming in and preparing my own order. At times I helped other customers, watched over always by the eagle eye of Mrs Mac. I enjoyed the shopkeeping routine, scooping out rice or beans or flour, weighing it then handing it to the customer. I became an even more frequent customer at Mr Mac's when I began running errands for our neighbour, Mrs Paul, to earn a few pennies with which to buy candies or save for a movie.

As I grew older and went to St Mary's College, I went less and less to Mr Mac's shop. He however always greeted me enthusiastically and announced my academic credentials to whoever was in the shop at the time. Going to University afterwards, I ceased going altogether, especially since I lived on campus at St Augustine for my first year. I found out several years later that my mother and younger sister had assumed the shopping duties, although on a more irregular schedule than had prevailed under my father. I noticed eventually that my mother stopped doing business at Mr Mac's; I never questioned why at the time, I simply assumed that she found the range and prices of goods elsewhere more attractive. I learned the truth many years later from my eldest brother.

In the 1970's Trinidad and Tobago was facing a foreign exchange crisis. The country had reverted to import controls.

Several items were placed on a Negative List by the government or were subject to strict import control. Potatoes were among the listed products. Shopkeepers hoarded these items, releasing them only to their regular customers. One day, my mother and sister went into the crowded shop and asked for potatoes.

'Them is Indian. We have no potatoes.' It was Mrs Mac, loudly, from her usual spot across the room.

My mother reddened and turned to leave. Mr Mac went behind her.

'Wait, I will get the potatoes for you,' said Mr Mac quietly.

It was too late. My mother left, never to step foot in Mr Mac's shop again. Whenever she needed anything, she always told us to go to the Chinese shop, or one of the two 'supermarkets', Low Budget or Rodrigues.

She never explained why to me, and I never asked. I got the story from my older brother only after my mother passed away many years later. Ignorant of the episode, I continued to say 'Good Morning' to Mr Mac and his wife whenever I saw them on a Sunday morning going to church. Even if I had known, I am not sure it would have made a difference.

Made in the USA
Columbia, SC
14 August 2022

64592026R00104